"Oh, no," Joe mu——
"Anything bu——

Wishbone and Joe stared —— ——doned Murphy house. Joe looked down at the clue he held in his hand. Sam and David stood on either side of him.

"This isn't good," Joe said in a low voice.

Bang! Everyone jumped as a broken shutter hit the peeling side of the house. The old Murphy place loomed silently before them again, hidden almost completely by shadows and overgrown weeds.

"Okay," Wishbone said. "Is it me, or did things just get really spooky?"

"Quick, guys! Let's go!" Sam dashed through the broken-down gate and went into the overgrown yard. Looking back, she said, "What are you waiting for?"

Wishbone, David, and Joe stood on the pavement, looking at her.

Finally Joe answered, "I can't."

Sam looked puzzled. "What do you mean, you can't?"

"It's  haunted," David explained. "The house is haunted."

The SUPER Adventures of WISHBONE™

The Legend of Sleepy Hollow

by Carla Jablonski

Screenplay by Jonathan Cuba, Rick Duffield,
and Michael Anthony Steele

Inspired by **"The Legend of Sleepy Hollow"**
by Washington Irving

WISHBONE™ created by Rick Duffield

SCHOLASTIC INC.

New York Toronto London Auckland Sydney
Mexico City New Delhi Hong Kong

ISBN 0-439-12919-2

12 11 10 9 8 7 6 5 4 3 2   9/9 0 1 2 3 4/0

Printed in the U.S.A.   40

First Scholastic printing, September 1999

Edited by Pam Pollack
Copy edited by Jonathon Brodman
Cover design by Lyle Miller
Interior illustrations by Don Punchatz
Wishbone photograph by Carol Kaelson

For Beth and Don, with thanks!

FROM THE BIG RED CHAIR . . .

Oh . . . hi! Wishbone here. You caught me right in the middle of some of my favorite things—books. Let me welcome you to THE SUPER ADVENTURES OF WISHBONE. In each of these books, I have adventures with my friends in Oakdale and imagine myself as a character in one of the greatest stories of all time. This story takes place in the fall, when Joe is fourteen, and he and his friends are in the eighth grade—during the second season of my television show. In *THE LEGEND OF SLEEPY HOLLOW*, I imagine I'm Ichabod Crane, the schoolteacher from Washington Irving's very spooky ghost tale, "**THE LEGEND OF SLEEPY HOLLOW.**" It is a story about superstitions and one of the most famous ghosts of all time, the Headless Horseman!

You're in for a real treat, so pull up a chair and a snack and enjoy *THE LEGEND OF SLEEPY HOLLOW!*

Chapter One

Wishbone raised his nose into the air and took in a big sniff. "Ah, yes!" The white-with-brown-and-black-spots Jack Russell terrier let out a deep, happy sigh. "There's nothing better than taking Wishbone for a nice long walk on a crisp autumn day—even if Wishbone has to do it himself."

Wishbone trotted along the streets of Oakdale and chased the blowing leaves. Wishbone could smell adventure just around the corner—and he was one dog with a super nose for adventure!

He headed toward Oak Street. People hurried by all around him. Wishbone wondered if they also felt the same sense of adventure in their bones—and were quickly on their way around town to find it!

"Helllooo, Oakdale!" Wishbone said. "I can't put my nose on it, but something strange is in the air. . . ."

Wishbone looked up and down the busy street. His eyes landed on a skeleton that was hanging in the front door of a store.

"Whoa! That guy has been waiting way too long for his order! And why are there so many pictures of black cats in all the store windows?" He shook his head. "Why would anyone purposely surround themselves with pictures of cats?" In one store window, masks of all kinds stared out at him. Their hollow eye slots were dark and mysterious.

Wishbone shivered as the autumn wind picked up again, whistling through the tree branches. A sudden gust blew a hat along the sidewalk in front of him. *I guess that hat decided to walk itself, too!* "I recommend that you get a leash for that hat," Wishbone told the man running toward him.

Wishbone continued down the street.

"*Brr!* What is it about today?" Red and gold leaves flipped over and over in front of him as he trotted along. "Look at that! The leaves are learning to dance."

The dog passed several houses and looked closely at them. Someone's laundry flapped on a backyard clothesline.

"The sheets are learning to fly!"

Pumpkins carved with jagged teeth and big hollow eyes grinned crookedly at him from the step of a porch.

"Pumpkins are suddenly growing faces."

Wishbone turned and faced the street again.

"There's no doubt about it," he said. "Something is in the air, something that makes people do the strangest things . . . something—"

Suddenly, Wishbone's whiskers went stiff. His head whipped around, looking back in the direction from where he came. His snack meter clicked on, ready for action.

"Something . . . *edible!*"

Wishbone's powerful sense of smell told him freshly baked cookies were being taken out of an oven. He sniffed deeply, zeroing in on the exact location. *Bingo!* The Talbots' house. *Yes!* His very own house had mouth-watering cookies in it! Fresh and chewy, soft and warm, straight out of the oven.

Wishbone's ears pricked up. He could hear the faint scraping sound of Ellen's spatula against one of the cookie sheets. Was one of those cookies sliding . . . sliding . . . ?

Yes! The cookie is slipping off the spatula—and flying toward the floor!

"Gotta go! Gotta go! Gotta go!" Wishbone raced down the street. He leaped over a stack of boxes piled by the curbside, hung a sharp left, and darted into the alley.

His four paws pounded the dirt and his heart thumped hard in his furred white chest. He ran as fast as he could down the alley toward home.

"Home and cookies!" *You're almost there,* he urged himself. He suddenly saw his next-door neighbor, Wanda Gilmore, kneeling in one of her gardens.

I can already see my house! Wishbone dashed across Wanda's yard and leaped over his startled neighbor's feet.

"Hi, Wanda! Can't stop to chat," Wishbone said over his shoulder. "Got a date with destiny!"

"Wishbone?" Wanda called after him.

"Cookie! Cookie! Cookie!" he repeated.

The little dog tore around the corner of his house to the back door. The cookie smell was even stronger now.

"Open door! Open door! Open door!" Wishbone tugged on the knotted rope that pulled the door open and dashed onto the screened-in back porch. He whirled around. "Close door. Close door. Close door." He tugged the rope hanging on the inside door to shut it. Then he flew through his doggie door, into the kitchen, ground zero, and placed himself right under the falling cookie.

It landed neatly in his mouth.

Gotcha! "Mmm-mmm! Good cookie!" Wishbone munched happily.

Ellen glanced down from where she stood at the counter. She was moving the cookies from the baking sheets to a cooling rack. She wore jeans and a black sweat shirt with a grinning jack-o'-lantern on the front. "Well, hello, Wishbone. Where did you just come from?"

Wishbone swallowed with a gulp. Then he licked the crumbs from his whiskers. "Excellent pumpkin cookie," he complimented Ellen. "New recipe?"

Before Ellen could answer, the back door banged open. Joe Talbot stepped into the kitchen. Joe, who was in the eighth grade, was Wishbone's very best friend. The brown-haired boy carried a gym bag. Wishbone recognized the hooded sweat shirt on Joe as the boy's favorite. He also sensed a very powerful smell the moment his best friend entered. *Sweat? Dirt? Sweaty dirt?*

"Wishbone, where have you been?" Joe asked. "Today was the very first day of basketball practice, and you weren't there. It's bad luck, especially today."

"Bad luck? Me?" *How strange! The cute little dog usually brings good luck.*

Wishbone trotted after his friend. Joe pulled the refrigerator door open and took out a soft drink. He twisted off the cap, then tilted his head back and took a long drink.

"Why is it so important that Wishbone be at your practice?" Ellen asked.

"My question exactly," Wishbone said. *And what* is *that smell?*

12

Joe set the soft-drink bottle on the counter near the sink. "Wishbone always comes to practice." The boy leaned against the counter and looked down at Wishbone. "You should have been there," Joe said. "It's a bad sign. I don't want to jinx the season!"

"I know I'm like a good-luck charm, but I didn't realize I was so important," Wishbone said. He took another sniff. *Something definitely reeks in this vicinity. Hmm . . . Sweat, dirt, locker room—and feet!*

Ellen took off her padded oven mitts and went over to Joe. "Your father was the same way when he was a coach. He was so superstitious about the start of basketball season. I can remember one time when he—" Ellen stopped talking, and her nose wrinkled. "What *is* that smell?" she asked. She looked around the kitchen.

"I think I just found the culprit, Ellen." Wishbone pawed at one of Joe's sneakers. "Don't look now, Joe, but there's something in your shoe!"

Ellen looked down. "Joe, why is Wishbone so interested in your sneakers?"

Joe grinned and lowered his head. "Sorry, Mom," he said. "They're my practice socks. My lucky ones."

Wishbone backed away from Joe's feet. *"Ewwww!* Didn't I bury those last year?"

"I think they're a little past their prime, Joe," Ellen said. She covered her nose with her hand and smiled. "But since they're so special, why don't you take them off and find a special place to put them? *Outside* the house," she added.

"If you want, I'll stash them with the new squeaky toy I just buried," Wishbone offered.

"I will, Mom," Joe replied. "But right now I need to go downtown to pick out a new basketball."

"You do?" Ellen asked, raising an eyebrow.

"Yes! We've already started this season's practice, Mom," Joe explained. "I can't begin a new year without a new ball. It's bad luck."

Ellen shook her head, then smiled. "Of course. I forgot."

Joe grinned. "Don't worry. I still have my birthday money. Besides, I want to check out the new equipment at the sporting-goods store." Joe headed for the back door. "Come on, Wishbone."

"But Joe," Wishbone objected. "Ellen might drop another cookie any minute. And they're pumpkin cookies. With icing faces!"

Ellen touched the cookies on the rack to see if they were cool enough to put into the cookie jar. "Have you decided whether or not you're going trick-or-treating?" she asked.

Wishbone sat up on his hind legs. He raised his front paws in the air. "Treating? I vote that we go for treats!"

Joe slouched over and shoved his hands into his pockets. "I don't think so," he replied. "I'll probably just stay home this year." Then he straightened up and zipped up his sweat shirt. He held open the door. "Come on, Wishbone. Let's go."

"But . . . cookies, Joe. . . . Well, okay." He trotted after his buddy. "Don't eat all the cookies while we're gone, Ellen!" the dog called to her on his way out the door.

The two pals ran quickly side by side. Joe fished a small blue ball out of his sweat shirt pocket. "Want to have a game of catch, boy?" he asked.

Wishbone leaped up. All four paws left the ground and he flipped in the air. "You bet! Throw me a long one, Joe!"

Joe pulled back his arm and then let the blue ball fly. Wishbone kept his eyes glued on it as it soared high above him. He took off.

Wishbone dove headfirst into a deep pile of dry, crackling leaves. *That ball can't hide from me.* Gripping the ball tightly in his teeth, the terrier popped his head up until it was clear of the pile. "Ta-da!" he cheered. He set the ball down. "You're right, Joe. This is as much fun as eating cookies." He leaped out of the pile, scattering leaves everywhere. "Well . . . almost," he added.

He gave his body a thorough shaking, picked up the ball, then ran back to Joe. Joe took the ball from Wishbone and let it sail again. Wishbone spun around and raced after it.

"I got it! I got it!" With his eyes on the ball, Wishbone dashed through a weather-beaten gate falling off its hinges and into a yard filled with weeds.

"Wishbone, wait! No!" Joe called behind him. "That's the Murphy house!"

Sorry, Joe, Wishbone thought. *I'll be with you in a second. Right now, I have a ball to catch!* The ball was coming down in a long, sweeping arc. "I have you now, Mr. Ball. You don't stand a chance of escaping from me!"

The ball was going to land right . . . over . . .

Wishbone stopped short. "Helllooo! What have we here?"

Two yellow eyes gleamed at him between

the strands of tall weeds. Then, with a rustling sound, the overgrown grass parted and a black cat dashed up onto the sagging porch.

"Ah, it's a cat." *That cat made me miss the catch of the century. Now, where is that ball?*

"Wishbone, come on!"

Wishbone looked back at Joe. For some reason, his friend was still standing on the other side of the gate. It was as if Joe didn't want to come any closer. *He must have seen the cat,* Wishbone figured. *I can't blame Joe for wanting to avoid a cat.*

Wishbone turned back. *Huh? Where did that cat go? He was just there! Wasn't he? Could I have only imagined that I saw him?* He looked back to Joe. "You didn't see where that cat went, did you, Joe?"

"Come on, Wishbone. Let's get out of here. I don't like this place."

Wishbone nosed around for the ball. He finally found it, then picked it up in his teeth and left the overgrown yard. The dog followed Joe a few steps along the pavement. Then he stopped and looked back at the house. It was an old, run-down two-story structure, gray, rain-stained, and lonely looking. The windows were boarded over. Some of the boards had cracked, split, or fallen off.

The sun was beginning to set behind the slanting roof. It sent strange, ghostly shadows

17

dancing along the broken shingles. A strong wind whistled in the bare trees, their scraggly branches reaching . . . reaching . . .

Wishbone shivered. "You're right, Joe. Places like this can play tricks on your mind. They cast a spell over you—a spell like the one that hung over a place called Sleepy Hollow."

Sleepy Hollow. Even the name sounds like a perfect place for a ghost story. Way back in 1819, American author Washington Irving wrote a short story called "The Legend of Sleepy Hollow." It took place not long after the American Revolution (1775–1783).

A strange atmosphere surrounded the little valley of Sleepy Hollow, New York. Washington Irving wrote that everyone who lived there, or spent any time there as a visitor, would breathe in the bewitching influence of the air. They would begin to hear strange sounds and see frightful apparitions—ghosts. All people in the area would fall under the spell of Sleepy Hollow.

This was something that the new Sleepy Hollow schoolmaster, Ichabod Crane, would soon find out. . . .

Chapter Two

Wishbone imagined he was Ichabod Crane, a schoolteacher who had read all about the latest superstitions, omens, and ghost stories. He pictured the early eighteenth-century Dutch farming community alongside the Hudson River where Ichabod was the new schoolmaster. He could see himself wearing the traditional three-cornered hat over his floppy ears. He had on a cutaway coat, which was a long jacket with a split back. That was the style for gentlemen of the time.

It was a long walk to the schoolhouse from the Van Ripper farm, where Ichabod was staying. His journey took him through the groves of walnut trees, over a little bridge, and past a church sitting next to the cemetery. He hurried by the silent gravestones, thinking of the ghosts that might appear each night at midnight, the witching hour. . . .

Ding! Ding! Ding! Ding! Ichabod Crane held the school bell firmly in his teeth and shook it with all his strength. He was calling the children to school. He stood outside the small log building, counting his pupils as they greeted him and went inside.

"Hurry, please," he urged. "Don't be tardy.

We may be right near Tarry Town, but there will be no tarrying here!"

Ichabod sounded strict, but his bark was far worse than his bite. He knew the children traveled quite a distance to attend school, and they were sometimes late.

The roughly built little schoolhouse was only a single room. The ceiling was high, and several of the windows were missing their panes of glass. Pages of some old schoolbooks with scribbled lessons on them were used in place of real windowpanes.

The schoolhouse sat at the foot of a tree-covered hill, off a small dirt path, with a small stream running behind it. It was quite a distance from the main road. It was as if a hush floated over the area. The place seemed almost . . . haunted.

Ichabod shivered. *Yes, there is something spooky about this little school out here all by itself.*

Now that the children were arriving, their cheerful voices filled the air.

Ichabod walked to the front steps of the schoolhouse. He turned and watched the last of the late-comers dash down the hill. He barked sharply, and the two boys and their sister hurried faster. Ichabod nipped at their heels as they ran into the schoolhouse. "This flock is a handful to herd," he said.

Ichabod glanced around one last time. Then he took a deep breath. He had to admit, the first week of school made him a little nervous. As a traveling schoolmaster, Ichabod moved from village to village. He met new students with each different teaching assignment he got. But Ichabod knew that his talent of telling ghostly tales and his skill at games quickly won the respect of even the most uninterested student.

It doesn't hurt to be cute, either! Ichabod thought, as he used his hind leg to scratch an itch under his chin. *And this old dog can certainly teach these kids some new tricks.*

Far more important to Ichabod than the three "R's"—reading, 'riting, and 'rithmetic— was the teaching only he could give. He felt that it was his most important duty to teach the reading of signs and symbols, and all the ways one could protect oneself against attacks of the supernatural.

And I have arrived here none too soon, Ichabod thought. *I have never seen a valley so full of magic.*

Ichabod stepped into the schoolhouse, eager to share his very special wisdom. As soon as the children noticed their schoolmaster entering, they hurried to sit in their seats. The youngest children sat up front, the oldest in the seats at the back. They slid into their benches and folded their hands on top of the long wooden desks they shared.

Ichabod leaped up onto his desk at the front of the room. He sat back on his haunches and gazed out at his pupils. There were fifteen students today, ranging in age from six to sixteen. *A good number,* Ichabod thought. Often, children had to stay at home to help with farm chores. For this reason, school attendance went up and down, changing with the seasons, and even from day to day.

"Good morning, students," he said.

"Good morning, teacher," the class answered together.

Ichabod waited as the children laid their copybooks—books with examples of handwriting to be copied in learning to write—on the desks. The oldest students filled their inkwells with their homemade ink, and they held on tightly to their hand-carved quill pens, ready to write. The younger children also had copybooks, but they wrote with bits of lead pencil. *Less messy that way,* Ichabod thought.

Once Ichabod saw that all his students were ready, he spoke to the class.

"It is a good thing I came to Sleepy Hollow," Ichabod told the children. "For this is a place that seems to be quite bewitched." In the short time since he had moved to Sleepy Hollow, New York, Ichabod was quite sure that he had seen more shooting stars and meteors than he had ever witnessed in his entire life in Connecticut.

"And you are the best schoolmaster we have ever had for a game of catch!" Philip Van Brock called from the back of the room.

"And you are excellent in races, too," Sarah Breuhofftin added.

Ichabod lowered his head, fearing his red face would be visible.

Tail wagging, Ichabod continued. "Thank you. Now, children," he said, "it is very important to know the difference between true knowledge and useless information."

Philip raised his hand. "How do we know the difference?"

Ichabod's tail wagged harder. "Very good question, young man. That is exactly what I am here to explain! To *tell* you the difference. For example, it is too bad the young farmer Jebediah didn't know that after you break a mirror, you must walk in a circle to reverse your bad luck. Clockwise, mind you."

Ichabod demonstrated by trotting in a circle on top of the desk.

"If Jebediah had listened to me, his cows would not have stopped giving milk, and his crops would not have failed. However, be very careful. This action is useless in the event of a different bit of bad luck!"

"What bad luck must we guard against?" Philip asked, his voice trembling.

"That is the unlucky event of having a black cat cross your path," Ichabod replied.

Ichabod stopped in mid-circle and shuddered. Cats! Just thinking of those creatures made his fur bristle.

"In that case," he instructed, "you must *not* walk clockwise, but circle counterclockwise— like this." Ichabod changed his direction and circled to the left. "Oh! And do so twice on Sundays!"

A blond boy wearing a blue shirt, wool trousers, and a three-cornered hat raised his hand.

"Yes, Andrew?" Ichabod asked.

"Excuse me, Mr. Crane," the ten-year-old said, "but my mother wants to know if you can come over to our house and finish the story about the secret of the full moon. She made your favorite apple pie."

Ichabod's ears pricked up. "Apple pie, you say?" He leaped off the desk and trotted over to Andrew. He stood up on his hind legs and leaned his paws on the front of the boy's wooden desk. "Why, of course. I'll come over, Andrew. Your mother's apple pie is the very finest in the county." Ichabod licked his chops. "I recall one Sunday . . ." His students stared silently back at him.

Whoops! I got a little carried away there. Thinking about food can do that to me!

Ichabod cleared his throat. "Oh . . . yes . . . Where were we?" He trotted back up to his desk.

"Ahem!" he said, clearing his throat once again. "Now, then. Eyes forward, everyone. Let's get back to our important lessons. Now, who knows why we ring a bell to begin each day?"

Ichabod's tail wagged with pride as he saw the many hands shoot up into the air. *What clever children these are. And they have been my students for only a week. Already I have worked miracles!*

"Yes, Elizabeth?" Ichabod said.

Elizabeth got off her bench and stood beside her desk. She wound her fingers through the long strings of her white bonnet. "Do you ring the bell to call us into the classroom?" she asked.

Ichabod's tail stopped wagging immediately. "No, no, no! Not at all." He shook his head. "We ring the bell to drive away demons and spirits." He placed a paw on the brass bell that sat on his desk. "It is a well-known fact that witches won't go near things made of brass. Also, ghouls and goblins hate the sound of bells."

Ichabod stood firmly on his four legs and forcefully shook his body. The little bell hanging from a button on his vest rang softly.

"Why do you think I wear this bell at all times?" the schoolmaster asked.

A murmur spread through the one-room

schoolhouse, and several children nodded. Satisfied that he had made his point, Ichabod then moved on to the next matter of the day.

"Now it is time to read and recite," he told the class. "Please open your books to page two. Everyone? Begin!"

The children bent over the books that they shared. Ichabod listened to them read aloud together. As the hours passed, he watched the journey of the sun through the schoolroom windows. It cast long shadows across the children's coats, which hung from pegs on the plain, bare walls. Pretty soon, Ichabod's stomach growled. Finally, finally, the long school day was over.

"Dismissed!" Ichabod announced. He darted in and out between his students' legs as they all raced out of the schoolhouse. "Excuse me! Pardon me! Coming through!" he called. *Ready or not, apple pie, here I come!*

"Mr. Crane," Andrew called, "do you want to play hoops?" The boy stood nearby, holding the large hoop and the stick he would use to spin it. He smiled at Ichabod.

"No!" Elizabeth protested. "Mr. Crane would much rather play hopscotch with us!"

"I'm afraid that I cannot play this afternoon. It will have to wait for another day,"

Ichabod answered. "I can't keep Andrew's pie—er . . . mother—waiting!"

Ichabod trotted along the trail leading away from the schoolhouse. Fallen autumn leaves crunched under his paws. He headed eagerly for Andrew's family's farm—and Andrew's mother's famous apple pie.

It will be a pleasure to live at Andrew's house at a later date, Ichabod thought. Having no permanent home of his own, Ichabod stayed with the families of the students he taught. As was the custom, he moved each week, carrying his few belongings wrapped in a scarf dangling from his teeth. He didn't mind. It was a good way to get to know his neighbors. Some of them were excellent cooks! Unfortunately, his current host, Mr. Van Ripper, was not one of them.

To pass the time on his walk, Ichabod decided to exercise his voice. It was his way to prepare for the singing lessons he was to teach later in the week. "Mee-mee-mee-mee-mee!" Ichabod's howl boomed and echoed through the woods.

"Caw! Caw!" A sudden rush of wings startled Ichabod. He glanced up to see dozens of chattering birds rise from the many bare tree branches.

"Mee-mee-mee-mee!" he sang out. More birds flew away.

How strange, Ichabod thought. *Every time I raise my voice in song, the birds take flight. Could this be another example of the bewitching of Sleepy Hollow?*

Ichabod smelled Andrew's family's farm before he saw it. *Mmm-mmm! It sure smells good. Yes,* he thought, *the meals I eat will improve once I move in here!*

"Hello!" he called as he entered the farmhouse. He let his nose lead him straight to the kitchen.

"Hello, Mr. Crane," Andrew's mother greeted him. She stood by the open fire in the big fireplace. She was stirring a kettle that hung low from a hook over the flames. "Make yourself at home," she added. She nodded toward the large wooden table in the center of the room.

Don't mind if I do! Ichabod leaped up onto the bench in front of the table. "Andrew tells me you wanted to hear more about the secret of the full moon."

"Yes, indeed, I do!" the woman exclaimed. "I want to be sure all the signs are favorable for our next planting season."

"I will be happy to check on that in my

30

almanac," Ichabod told her. His tail thumped against the back of the hard wooden bench as he watched the woman cut a large piece of apple pie.

"Now, tell me, Ichabod," she continued, setting a plateful of the mouth-watering pie in front of him. "What would your author Cotton Mather have to say about Sleepy Hollow's Hessian ghost?"

Cotton Mather was the great scholar who wrote Ichabod's favorite book, *The History of Witchcraft in New England.* He knew almost every page by heart. Ichabod licked pie crumbs off his whiskers, then said, "I have not heard of a Hessian ghost."

Andrew's mother's eyes widened. "No one has told you of the terrifying ghost of Sleepy Hollow? I am so surprised!"

Ichabod pushed the empty plate toward her with his nose. "Er . . . perhaps hearing the story will require the strength I will get only by eating a second helping of pie."

Andrew's mother cut another piece of pie for Ichabod. Then she sat across the table from him and gazed into his eyes. "There have been many who have seen this frightening spirit," she whispered, as if the ghost might hear her and decide to make an appearance right there in the farmhouse kitchen. "In fact, I believe he is the most feared of all the ghosts that live in Sleepy Hollow."

Ichabod nodded. "The head honcho of all the ghosts of the air, you might say?"

"Oh, yes!" Andrew's mother exclaimed. "That's it—*exactly!*"

Ichabod shivered. Then he urged the woman to continue. "I must know everything," he told her. "Don't leave out a single detail."

"On many a moonlit night, travelers heading through Sleepy Hollow have seen a terrifying figure on horseback," she told him. "A rider without a head!"

Ichabod gasped. He nearly choked on the last bite of his pie. "A headless horseman? Here?"

Andrew's mother nodded. "It is said that it is the ghost of a German soldier who was hired by England to fight against us during the Revolutionary War. This Hessian soldier's head was blown off by cannonball fire. His body lies buried in the churchyard cemetery," she said quietly.

"But why does he ride?" Ichabod asked. He pushed the plate across the table once more. Andrew's mother absently got up and brought more pie over. This time she didn't bother to cut just a single piece. She simply set what was left of the pie in front of Ichabod.

She glanced around and lowered her voice even more. "I believe he is out searching for a new head! And he must always return to his grave before daybreak."

Ichabod could feel his heart thumping under his fur. *What a story! This is what I feared!* "I had not heard about this ghost," he said. "As I must cross Sleepy Hollow every evening, I will keep a sharp eye and ear out for this creature." He patted his three-cornered hat with his paw. "I am quite attached to my head, you see."

"Just remember," the woman warned Ichabod. "The Headless Horseman not only haunts the valley, but the nearby roads, too. He especially likes the area near the church."

"I shall take very special care," Ichabod promised.

Finally, it was time for Ichabod to return to the Van Ripper farm, where he was staying that week. The sun had set hours ago. Ichabod's journey would take him past the cemetery where the Hessian's headless body lay buried.

Ichabod's fur bristled in the cool night air. His whiskers twitched at every odd scent. His ears pricked up at each new sound.

What's that? Ichabod whipped his head around. He scanned the area closely. *Were those twigs crackling under someone's feet—or hooves? Is someone following me?* "Come out, come out, wherever you are!" Ichabod called. However, he really, really hoped no one would answer.

When Ichabod got no response, he continued cautiously on his way. He knew the witching hour would soon be upon him. *What if I am still in the dark woods at that dreadful hour?* he worried. *The only light to guide my path will be the pale moon. Shall I be hounded by ghosts of every kind?*

The schoolmaster's legs picked up speed. The call of the whippoorwill, the hooting of the screech owl, and the sudden flurry of squawking birds frightened from their roosts all joined in to hurry him along his route.

"Aargh!" he cried, as something flew into his face. "What is that?" *Oh . . . just a lightning bug,* he told himself. *Don't bug out now!* He felt his heart slowly return to its normal beating.

He finally saw the flickering candlelight glowing in a window of the Van Ripper farmhouse. With a cheerful bark, Ichabod trotted across the yard and went to the door. He glanced one last time into the dark night. *Well done,* he congratulated himself. *Those ghosts*

know to stay clear of this schoolteacher, for they know I am on to their clever ways. They have met their match in me!

Ichabod has ghosts and ghouls to worry about.

I have that black cat I want to keep track of!

Chapter Three

Wishbone took a quick glance back toward the Murphy house and shivered. *That is one spooky place,* he thought. *It's the perfect hangout for a black cat.* "I guess you didn't like that black cat, either, huh, Joe?" Wishbone asked, as he trotted alongside his friend.

Soon the two arrived at the new sporting-goods store, Oakdale Sports & Games. The cool, two-story building had once been the old firehouse. Halloween banners hung from the second story, flapping in the breeze. Wishbone ran ahead, past the bicycle racks and toward the large front doors.

Joe and Wishbone stood aside to allow a group of kids to come out of the doors. Just inside the front entrance, Wishbone noticed a display of tennis balls. "Dog toys!" he said with glee.

"Stay outside, Wishbone. I won't be long," Joe said, as he walked inside.

Wishbone sneaked into the store right behind Joe. Colorful posters lined the walls. Racks with games, sports equipment, and athletic clothing stood scattered throughout the large store. Wishbone ran across the floor and leaped into a huge bin of bright yellow balls. A moment later, his head popped up, a tennis ball in his teeth.

"I think I found the perfect one!" Then he let the ball drop. "But I'd better test them all— just to be sure." He dove back down.

Wishbone came up again from under the pile of balls. He scanned the large store, looking for Joe. *Hmm . . . I see display cases, stacks of sports equipment, and— Oh, there he is. I should have known.*

Wishbone jumped out of the bin and headed over to an area set up with a basketball hoop. Joe was just about to try a free throw from the foul line.

"Okay, Joe, do it just the way I showed you," Wishbone coached, sitting at the sideline. *Hey, cool!* he thought, as he settled onto the bright green artificial grass that covered both sides of the basketball court. *Indoor grass!*

Wishbone could see his buddy narrow his eyes, concentrating. Then Joe let the ball fly. It hit the rim and bounced off.

Whoop! Whoop! Whoop! Whoop!

"Aaaah!" Wishbone cried out, as he lay down and lowered his head.

Loud sirens blared and big bright red lights flashed inside the store. Joe quickly put the basketball back on the display rack.

"Are we going to be arrested?" Wishbone asked, scrambling to his feet. "Wow! Talk about a penalty shot!"

Joe looked around. "What's going on?" he said.

The sirens stopped screeching, and the red lights stopped flashing. Travis Del Rio, a dark-haired man in his thirties, walked over. He wore a green Oakdale Sports & Games T-shirt, and blue jeans. "We have another victim," he said with a friendly grin. He pointed to a sign hanging over the basketball hoop.

"'The Haunted Rim,'" Joe read. "'Shoot at your own risk.'" Joe shook his head. "I guess I'm a little off today, Mr. Del Rio."

"Well, Joe, it happens to the best of players," he told Joe, clapping him on the back. Travis smiled as he gazed back up at the basket. "But there's nothing like the thrill of being in the zone— where the hoop looks three feet wide and everything you toss up goes in the basket." He gave Joe a broad smile. "I'm sure you'll be there again, Joe."

"Thanks, Mr. Del Rio," Joe said. "I hope you're right."

"I know I am." Travis clapped a hand on Joe's back again. Then he sniffed deeply. "Do you smell something?"

Joe shrugged and shook his head.

Travis glanced down at Wishbone.

"Don't look at me," Wishbone said.

"Hi, Wishbone. How are you doing, boy?" asked Travis.

"Can't complain," Wishbone replied. "Not when I'm surrounded by all this great stuff!"

Joe took a quick look down. "Hey, Wishbone. Where did you come from? I thought you were waiting outside."

"I'm not surprised to see him," Travis said. "After all, I bet Wishbone enjoys sports and games as much as we do! He's always welcome in here."

"I knew you were my kind of guy," Wishbone replied. "I could tell by your collection of dog toys."

"Well, Joe, what can I do for you?" Travis asked. "What can I show you today?"

That's my cue! "Okay, Joe." Wishbone sat up on his haunches. "Can we discuss toys? How about tennis balls? Just all the yellow ones."

A movement behind them caused Wishbone to whirl around.

"Express ride down!" the dog exclaimed, as Travis's niece and nephew slid, one by one, down a pole from the second floor. Wishbone knew they had recently come to live with their uncle in Oakdale.

"That old fire pole is really cool," Joe said.

"Can they do the same trick going up?" Wishbone asked, peering up at the ceiling.

Travis grinned and nodded. "I'm glad we decided to keep the firefighters' pole when we made changes to the old firehouse. Since we made the upstairs our living area, it makes getting downstairs from the apartment a snap."

This place is always fun, Wishbone thought. *Everything a dog might ever want to play with is all under one roof. Entire bins of balls. Even a "haunted" basketball hoop! I wonder what other cool things Travis has around here.*

The two youngsters rushed toward Travis. "Uncle Travis," the girl called, "we need help with our costumes."

"Melina, Marcus," Travis said. "You know Joe Talbot, don't you?"

The eleven-year-old girl smoothed her long, straight brown hair behind her ears and smiled. "Yes, we do. Hi," she said.

"I bet it's fun living over the store," Joe said to Marcus.

The ten-year-old boy nodded. "I can zip downstairs and shoot hoops anytime I want!"

Travis ruffled the boy's dark hair. "As you can see, we're really enjoying Oakdale," Travis said.

"Have you guys checked out the tennis balls yet?" Wishbone asked.

Marcus bent over to pat Wishbone. When

he stood back up, he wrinkled his forehead. "Something smells funny," he complained.

"It's not the dog," Wishbone said. "Uh . . . Joe, do you want to handle this one?"

"So are you guys getting ready to go trick-or-treating tonight?" Joe asked.

Hmm . . . Do I detect a quick change of topic? Wishbone wondered.

"No! Even better than that!" Marcus said, his brown eyes sparkling with excitement. "Uncle Travis is letting us—"

"Marcus," Travis interrupted. "Why don't you go pick up those tennis balls and put them back where they belong?"

"Oh, okay. 'Bye!" The boy hurried over to the display.

"Have you signed up for the scavenger hunt yet?" Melina asked Joe.

"Scavenger hunt?" Joe repeated. "Oh, right. I heard about that."

Travis grinned. "If you liked my Haunted Rim, you'll really like my scavenger hunt."

"It's the best Halloween treat in Oakdale!" Melina exclaimed.

"Absolutely," Travis agreed. "And the first prize is a one-hundred-dollar gift certificate to the store."

Wishbone's ears pricked up. "How much is that in tennis balls, Joe?" he asked.

But Joe seemed to hesitate. "Well, I don't know . . ."

Travis walked over to the front counter and picked up a clipboard. "Come on," he insisted. "It's going to be fun!"

Joe followed Travis slowly over to the counter.

"I'm sure there's still room for you to join one of the teams."

Travis scanned the list on the clipboard. Melina pointed to a name on the list.

"Wait a minute," Travis said. "It's your lucky day! You're already signed up on Samantha Kepler's team."

"I am?" Joe asked, surprised. "I hadn't really decided yet."

"And her dad has even promised to supply pizza for the party afterward," Travis added.

"Mmm . . . I could go for a slice of Pepper Pete's pizza right now!" Wishbone wagged his tail. "This scavenger hunt is sounding better by the minute."

"Look, Mr. Del Rio, I'm not sure about this scavenger hunt . . ." Joe began.

"Huh?" Wishbone glanced up at his friend, surprised by Joe's hesitation.

"Don't worry, Joe," Travis said. "It—" Then he took another deep whiff. "What *is* that smell?"

"Uh . . . well . . ." Joe shrugged and looked at Travis. "It's my socks," he admitted. "You'll think this is strange, but I always wear the same pair of socks at practice—for good luck."

Travis held up a hand. "Say no more." He pointed to a glass display case behind the counter. Wishbone stood on his hind legs to peer inside. He saw a pair of beat-up track shoes sitting beside a trophy and a newspaper article featuring a photo of Travis.

"Wow!" Joe said, staring at the article. "You won a major relay event."

"He sure did!" Melina said, smiling at her uncle.

Travis nodded proudly. "Yes, I certainly did—wearing those very shoes. And, believe me, they are behind glass for a reason."

Hmm . . . People sure have odd good-luck charms, Wishbone observed.

"I competed in many different sports," Travis said.

"Joe, can Wishbone do any tricks?" Melina asked.

"Tricks?" Wishbone repeated. "That depends. Got any treats?"

I'm always ready for treats. But I know one guy whose appetite for the supernatural is even greater than his desire for food.

Chapter Four

"Oh, my! Oh, dear! My goodness! Indeed!" Ichabod Crane lay in a field under a big oak tree, reading his favorite book, Cotton Mather's *The History of Witchcraft in New England.* Although the air was cool, it wasn't the chill that made him shiver—it was fear. "Oh, what delicious, terrifying tale will Cotton Mather describe next?"

Ichabod's tail wagged happily as he eagerly turned the page.

"Of *course* the woman is a witch!" Ichabod insisted aloud, as if the page could hear him. "The sour milk! The mysterious winds! All the signs are there. Oh, will Cotton Mather realize what's going on in time?"

"Ahem!" Someone behind him cleared a throat.

Ichabod leaped to his four feet, dropping the book to the grass. "Oooh! Oh! Don't hurt me!" he cried, dashing behind the tree. He shook his furred body, so that the witch-warning bell he wore on his vest rang loudly.

A rosy-faced young woman stood in front of him. "My, you're a jumpy fellow," she said. She straightened her straw bonnet, then retied the pink ribbons that held it in place. She smiled, and Ichabod noticed a tiny dimple appear in each pink and plump cheek.

Ichabod came out from behind the tree trunk. He patted his vest and straightened his three-cornered hat with a paw. "What? Er . . . ah . . . Oh, yes. How do you do? My name is Ichabod Crane."

The woman's smile widened when she realized who he was. "Why, you must be the schoolteacher! I'm Katrina Van Tassel."

"Van Tassel, you say?" he repeated. "Of the Van Tassel farm?"

"Why, yes." She smoothed down the front of her long pink-and-white dress. Then she pulled the lacy shawl around her shoulders a little tighter.

Ichabod's tail wagged. He took a step closer to the woman. "That really big farm?"

"Yes," she said again.

"The really, *really* big farm?"

Katrina smiled and nodded.

Ichabod sat back on his haunches. "Let's cut to the chase here. I'm talking about the really, really, super-duper, big, *big* farm?"

Katrina laughed. "Yes. That's the one. I was just—"

Ichabod lowered his nose to his front paws in a deep bow. "I'm delighted to meet you, Miss Van Tassel."

"Why, thank you. I'm pleased to meet you, too," she replied. "We're lucky to have such an educated and cultured gentleman as you among us."

Ichabod could feel himself blush under his white fur. It was an honor to receive such a lovely compliment from such a lovely lady with such a lovely, food-producing farm.

Katrina bent down to pick up the book Ichabod had dropped. "What are you reading, Mr. Crane?" she asked.

Ichabod took the book back from her and turned it over. "This is Cotton Mather's book on witchcraft. Most fascinating."

"It must be quite exciting!" Katrina exclaimed. "I love stories of the supernatural. They are my favorite."

Ichabod gazed at Katrina, his tail wagging. *Why, she is as wise as she is pretty,* Ichabod thought. "Oh, yes, the supernatural is exciting!" he replied. "I would love to tell you all about it."

To Ichabod's embarrassment, his stomach chose that very moment to let out a loud growl. Katrina glanced sideways at him, and Ichabod blushed.

"Oh, dear." Ichabod patted his vest with his paw. "Was that my stomach? I confess, I am a bit hungry," he told her.

"Why, please come and have dinner with us, Mr. Crane," Katrina responded. "That way, you can tell me all about Mr. Mather's book on witchcraft."

This must be a lucky day for me, Ichabod thought. *I should have recognized the good sign when those rabbits ran alongside me this morning. That always means good fortune is about to come my way.* "What a marvelous idea, Katrina! May I call you Katrina?"

"Of course," she said.

"Shall we go?" Ichabod said.

Ichabod and Katrina walked through the woods to the Van Tassel farm.

"My father's farm is very large," Katrina explained as they followed the sparkling brook. "It begins here, and then it goes all the way down to the Hudson River."

Soon Ichabod could see the farmhouse up ahead. A large, three-story structure nestled cozily among a grove of trees beside the wide river. The house was white, built in the style of the first Dutch settlers. Ichabod could see its sharply sloping roof and brightly painted doors and shutters. Nearby stood a large barn bursting with all the crops grown on the farm. From where Ichabod stood, he could see drying wheat hanging from the ceiling inside. Songbirds twittered, and pigeons perched on the roof. Ichabod raised his ears, hearing the horses neighing in the stables.

As Ichabod and Katrina strolled along the path leading up to the house, chickens squawked and hurried out of their way. Women in aprons and bonnets, wearing slings filled with grain, nodded at the pair while tossing food to the birds. Armies of turkeys and hens gobbled their way through the yard.

Look at them all! Ichabod's mouth watered as he imagined all the omelets, soufflés, and fried, scrambled, and over-easy eggs those hens would provide in a single day! He could smell all the pigs, though he didn't see their pens. He

heard the cows mooing from their stalls in the big barn.

Ichabod aimed his round brown eyes across the fields and orchards. In his imagination, he didn't see the wheat and the fruit trees. In their place he pictured mouth-watering treats of freshly baked bread and rich, warm pies.

What a life it would be, he thought, *to be top dog of this place!*

Ichabod's whiskers twitched as he took in

all the delicious smells. They included, he
believed, the wonderful aroma of a tasty dinner
being prepared. He could smell it as he and
Katrina neared the house. His four legs moved a
little more quickly, urged on by the scent of
roasting meats.

Ichabod trotted after Katrina onto the wide
front porch. It ran in front of the farmhouse.
Benches had been built into the walls that ran
the length of the porch. Katrina greeted an old

woman churning butter at one end of the front porch.

Ichabod licked his chops. *I bet that butter will taste awfully good melting over some hot, freshly baked bread,* Ichabod thought.

There is nothing the Van Tassels cannot produce on this farm, Ichabod realized with admiration. *And quite deliciously!*

". . . and that's why I named the horse Thunder," Katrina was saying.

"Excuse me? Oh, yes, yes! Thunder. Er . . . and lightning." *I mustn't get too carried away thinking only about food,* Ichabod reminded himself.

"What?" Katrina looked puzzled.

"This is quite a place you have here," Ichabod said. He hoped Katrina didn't notice how distracted he had been. "Indeed, your family has been very lucky," Ichabod continued. "An estate this size hardly seems possible in such a frightful frontier area as this."

"Frightful?" Katrina sounded puzzled. "In what way?"

"Why, I mean all of the supernatural forces that are at work around here," Ichabod explained.

"Why, yes," Katrina agreed, her brow

wrinkling. "You must help us find ways to keep bad spirits out of our home."

"I certainly will!" Ichabod promised.

He gazed around the farm, looking for hints of any ghosts. He wasn't about to allow some sneaky spirit to gobble down even a single bite of all the wonderful food growing on the Van Tassel property.

As Katrina pushed open the heavy front door, Ichabod pointed above it. "You should start right there," he said.

"What do you mean?" Katrina asked.

"You must hang a horseshoe over the door," he told her. "Then your good luck will never leave you."

Katrina smiled. "I shall tell Father at once," she said. "What a relief to have such an expert as you in our little community."

Pleased to have been of service, Ichabod wagged his tail. As he and Katrina went into the house, he scanned the room for any other weaknesses in supernatural security. On first glance, he found none, but he was certain if he were allowed a second visit he could make sure.

"Mother," Katrina called. A plump woman entered from a room at the back. She wore a flour-covered apron over her bright blue wool dress.

"Why, Katrina," the woman said. "We've been wondering where you'd gone off to."

"I'm sorry, Mother," Katrina replied, "but I ran into our new schoolmaster during my walk. We took the long way home. I've invited him for dinner."

Ichabod trotted over toward Mrs. Van Tassel. "I'm delighted to meet you," Ichabod said. He lowered his nose to the ground in a quick bow.

"Well, hello!" Mrs. Van Tassel replied warmly. "I've been meaning to talk to you about signing up Katrina for singing lessons."

Ichabod's tail thumped hard. Having a new student meant he would earn extra money, and—even better—he would have extra chances to visit the Van Tassel farmhouse. Surrounded by all that food!

"I would be very happy to schedule lessons," Ichabod told the woman, his tail wagging with even more energy.

"Dinner will be ready any moment," Mrs. Van Tassel said. "We've already been bringing food to the table. Katrina, please show Mr. Crane into the dining room."

Ichabod sniffed the air. "Unless I miss my guess," he said, trotting ahead of the women, "I believe the dining room is right through here."

The two Van Tassel women laughed. "Right you are!" Katrina exclaimed. "Perhaps you have the gift of second sight."

"No, no," Ichabod replied. "But I do have the gift of second scent!"

Ichabod lay curled up by the fireplace in the Van Tassels' huge parlor. His tail was slowly thumping with pleasure. Dinner was over, and the family and guests had gone into the parlor to tell stories.

I'm warm, my stomach is full, and it's story time. Life doesn't get any better than this!

"Mr. Crane believes that Sleepy Hollow is quite haunted," Katrina said.

Ichabod sat up and scratched behind his ear with his hind leg. He noticed several of the dinner guests nodding.

"Why, yes," Ichabod said. "There have been many signs of the supernatural here."

"We certainly know that," agreed Mrs. Van Tassel. "We're quite surrounded by ghosts!"

"Now, now," Mr. Van Tassel said, patting his wife's hand. "It's not as bad as all that."

"Oh, but it is!" Ichabod whispered. He

gazed around the room, watching the eerie shadows from the fire flickering across the faces of the group. "Never underestimate the ghost population. If you do, you'll find yourself up to your ears in them." His own ears pricked up, just thinking about the possibility!

Ichabod joined Katrina on a bench.

"You must know about the Headless Horseman," the young woman said.

"Why, yes, of course!" Ichabod shivered, remembering Andrew's mother's chilling tale of the headless rider.

"But have you heard of Major Andre's ghost?" she asked.

"Tell me all about him!" Ichabod sat up on his haunches.

"Major Andre haunts the very woods around here." Katrina paused and waved toward the windows at the back of the house.

Ichabod shuddered, knowing they were the very same woods that stood between him and the Van Ripper farm.

"He was hanged as a spy," Katrina continued, "but he went to his death saying that what was happening to him was unfair. He claimed that Benedict Arnold, a traitor in the American Revolution, betrayed him. His ghost has been seen beside the very tree they hanged him from."

"He's waiting for Benedict Arnold's ghost so he can have his revenge," a farmer said.

Ichabod's fur bristled with fear. He wondered if the angry ghost might make the mistake of seeking revenge against a totally innocent person—such as a schoolmaster walking home alone.

"Most fascinating," Ichabod told Katrina.

"We should tell Ichabod about The Shrieking Woman in White," another guest suggested. "She haunts the dark, narrow valley at Raven Rock. She is often heard to scream out on winter nights before a storm. That valley is the spot where she disappeared in the snow."

Ichabod's heart pounded. *Raven Rock? Why, that sits right beside the schoolhouse. In fact, I shall be passing it on my way to the Van Ripper farmhouse! I knew Sleepy Hollow was under some sort of magic spell, but I had no idea it was completely overrun with ghosts!*

Katrina held up a hand to quiet the group. "Please, Ichabod," she said. "Tell us how Cotton Mather would deal with all these troublesome spirits."

Ichabod felt everyone's eyes upon him. He

straightened his vest with his paws, then cleared his throat. "Er . . . Ahem! . . . Yes. Well . . ."

Come on, Ichabod, he urged himself. *You can't keep your audience waiting.*

"Cotton Mather has had the most incredible meetings with spirits," Ichabod explained. "He describes the case of a very troublesome kind of spirit known as a poltergeist. A poltergeist likes to play pranks on people and make a lot of noise. This ghost stole the pen right out of a man's hand. Then it scattered ashes over the poor fellow's clothing, hit him on the head with a shoe, and made a dish jump into a pail and splash water all over him."

Ichabod shuddered. He never wanted to meet such a wild spirit. Then he had a scary thought—a thought that made his fur stand on end! What if just by retelling Cotton Mather's fur-tingling tales he might be making *himself* a target for a poltergeist?

From everything Ichabod had read, he knew that the spirits were easily insulted—even when a person did not mean to offend them. *Perhaps I should talk about a different part of Cotton Mather's teachings.*

"Among Mather's most important writings are his excellent studies on witches. Oh, the poor bewitched." Ichabod's voice trembled with emotion. But he couldn't stop now. He felt he had a duty to continue. Besides, a second helping of dessert might still be a possibility. . . .

"What happens to them?" Katrina whispered fearfully.

Ichabod gathered every bit of his strength to tell of the terrifying experiences of the bewitched. Then he noticed the sunset through the window. He leaped to his four feet. "Oh, my!" he cried.

His sudden movement startled his eager listeners. Mrs. Van Tassel let out a shrill cry and dropped her cup of tea. "What is it? Is it a ghost?" she shrieked.

"Oh, my, no," Ichabod told her. "Nothing like that. It's just that I noticed the sun is setting, and I like to return home before dark."

Mrs. Van Tassel's bright red face returned to its normal coloring, and the other guests let out sighs of relief. Ichabod gave his thanks for both the hospitality and the stories. Katrina stood and walked him to the door.

"Will you continue your stories over dinner tomorrow?" Katrina asked Ichabod.

Ichabod's tail wagged happily. "Dinner tomorrow? Well, if you insist," he replied.

Ichabod said good-bye to his kind hosts. Then he left the farmhouse and trotted along the lonely path toward home.

Ah, a delightful meal—and a return invitation. Ichabod smiled. *I think that went rather well.*

Leaves rustled in the wind, making his fur stand straight up. "What's that? Who's there?" *Major Andre? The Shrieking Woman in White. Oh, dear—could it be the Headless Horseman himself?* Ichabod whipped his head around, cocking his ears. He took in a deep breath. *It's only the wind,* he told himself. He continued along the path.

At the sound of an owl hooting, Ichabod jumped into the air and twirled around. He looked all over for any ghosts that might be hiding nearby. *I can't be caught out alone after dark,* he realized.

Well, they say that exercise is good for the legs," he said. "And I've got four of them! Come along, Ichabod."

He ran down the path, his bell ringing all the way.

And now, let's dash back to Oakdale. I am beginning to discover that the town is superstitious and also includes ghostly surprises.

Chapter Five

"Okay, Joe. Big throw this time." Wishbone raced ahead, then spun around. He waited for his friend to throw him the ball. But, to his surprise, Joe just bounced the blue ball up and down as they walked along the alley on their way home from Oakdale Sports & Games.

"What is it about this day, Wishbone?" Joe asked. He let the shopping bag with the basketball in it dangle from one hand. He used the other hand to bounce the small blue ball. "First, you weren't at basketball practice. Then I accidentally threw this ball into the front yard of the old Murphy place. Now I'm signed up for a scavenger hunt tonight. On Halloween—of all nights!" He bounced the ball harder, sending it higher.

"Come on, Joe, I'm wide open!" Wishbone

ran a few yards ahead on the sidewalk. Still, Joe didn't toss him the ball. "Oooh-kay. How about a *little* throw?"

"Last year on Halloween," Joe went on, "I sprained my ankle so badly that I couldn't play basketball for a month. The year before that, I had the chicken pox."

Wishbone watched the ball go up and down. Up and down. Up and down. "So I'm guessing a game of catch is out of the question at the moment, huh, Joe?"

"This year," Joe continued, walking ahead of Wishbone, "a Halloween prankster was on the loose last week, causing trouble for everyone."

"So you've got kind of a problem with Halloween," Wishbone said. "Now I get it."

Joe caught the ball and shoved it into the pocket of his sweat shirt. "I think I'm just going to stay home tonight, before anything else happens," he said.

"Whatever you want to do is fine with me," Wishbone told Joe. Then he ran right into Joe's legs as Joe came to a sudden stop. "Hey! What's up? Where's the red light?"

Joe stood frozen on the pavement. Then Wishbone noticed the black cat walking across their path.

"Oh . . . will you look at the nerve of that fur ball!" the dog complained.

"Oh, no," Joe said. "Can this day get any worse?"

Wishbone looked up at Joe in surprise. "It's just a cat, Joe," Wishbone said. "Let's go chase him!" Wishbone let out a warning bark, and the cat scurried away. "Come on, Joe! After him!" Wishbone ran after the cat, but then he realized something was missing—or, rather, *someone*.

Wishbone turned around. Joe still stood in the center of the sidewalk, shaking his head.

"Joe? Earth to Joe. Can you read me? Come in, Joe—Earth is calling."

"That's it," Joe said. "A black cat just crossed my path. Now I *know* this day is jinxed." The bag with the basketball in it banged back and forth against his leg. "I'd better not take any more chances."

"Mmm-mmm," Wishbone said, as he sat by the kitchen counter. "All this talk of tricks and treats is making me hungry."

Ellen poured some kibble into Wishbone's bowl. Then she set it down in front of him.

"Why, thank you, Ellen. Don't mind if I do!"

Ellen put the dog-food bag back into the cabinet. Then she washed her hands and carried a basket of biscuits over to the table. She sat down beside Joe to eat dinner.

"Are you sure you don't need help handing out treats tonight?" Joe asked.

Wishbone's ears pricked up. "Treats? Ding-ding-ding-ding! Congratulations, Joe. You just said the secret word. Ellen, tell him what he's won!"

"I'd love to have your company, Joe," Ellen said with a smile, "but I think I can handle it."

"Are you sure?" Joe asked. "There are going to be a lot of kids coming around."

"Joe, the scavenger hunt will be a lot of fun," Ellen told him. "You'll be with your friends. Sam's counting on you. You should go."

Joe leaned back into his chair and pushed his plate aside. "Halloween has always been unlucky for me," he admitted.

Wishbone trotted over to the table. He gazed up at Joe's uneaten dinner. "Uh . . . Joe, if you're not going to finish that . . . ?"

"We all wonder about our luck from time to time," Ellen said. "Your father wondered about his every time his players started missing free throws, but he never gave up on them. He wanted them to play *through* it."

Ellen gazed sympathetically at Joe.

"There's no way you can know what's going to happen tonight, or on any other day. Nobody can. If you expect the worst, though, you might just find it. I'm pretty sure you'll have a lot of fun tonight."

"I guess so . . ." Joe said.

Wishbone put his paws on Joe's legs and looked up at his pal's face. "Come on, buddy," he said, wagging his tail. "We're going to have a great time! And don't worry. I'll keep all those black cats away from you."

Joe patted Wishbone's head and smiled.

"I believe my work here is done," Wishbone said. He trotted back over to his bowl to finish his dinner.

Wishbone's fur stood on end as he trotted alongside Joe. Somehow this dusk seemed darker than usual. The houses they passed were lit only by flickering candles set inside grinning jack-o'-lanterns. Shadowy shapes whipped in and out, keeping Wishbone alert to every tiny movement he noticed.

"There they are, Joe!" Wishbone said with excitement, as he and Joe entered Oakdale Sports & Games for a second time that day. He spotted Samantha Kepler and David Barnes right away. They were Joe's best friends—right after Wishbone, of course.

Sam was dressed as an explorer-adventurer, in a khaki jungle outfit. Her long blond hair was under a pith helmet.

David was dressed as a mad scientist in a lab coat and a pair of glow-in-the-dark psychedelic glasses.

Yup, Wishbone thought as he and Joe approached them, *those costumes fit those two to a T!* Sam was as ready for adventure as Wishbone was, and David was a science whiz, building and inventing all kinds of interesting gadgets.

"Great costumes, you two," Joe said, greeting his friends. Joe was dressed as a SWAT-team commando. He wore a black turtleneck under green-and-brown camouflage fatigues. His hat had the same kind of camouflage pattern on it. He was also wearing heavy black army-style boots and black gloves. He looked ready to take on anything.

"Hi, Joe. Hi, Wishbone," David replied.

"Glad you came, Joe," Sam said.

Joe shrugged.

"He almost changed his mind three times," Wishbone said as he sat down, "but you didn't hear that from me."

Sam knelt down and scratched Wishbone behind the ears. "Hey, Wishbone," she said. "Where's your costume?"

Wishbone raised his head and sat up perfectly straight. "Huh? A dog wearing a silly costume? I don't think so."

"Nice costume, Talbot."

Wishbone glanced up at the familiar voice. "Uh-oh," he murmured. "Damont."

Damont Jones was also in the eighth grade at Sequoyah Middle School. He and Joe were strong competitors on the basketball court. Sometimes it seemed that Damont took that rivalry off the court as well. He was wearing a black T-shirt, jeans, and a hat sitting low on his head. With Damont was his nine-year-old cousin, Jimmy. Jimmy was dressed all in silver, with antennae on his head.

"Hey, Damont," Joe said. "What are you supposed to be?"

"Your worst nightmare," Damont replied.

He turned to Sam. "Are you here to watch me win that gift certificate?"

"Yeah," Jimmy piped up, "we're going to win because I used to go on scavenger hunts all the time—"

"Can it, Jimmy," Damont interrupted. "You may be my cousin, but you're here only because my mom made me bring you."

"Jimmy, what are you dressed as?" Sam asked, ignoring Damont.

"A potato ready to be popped into the oven?" Wishbone guessed.

"I'm an alien," Jimmy announced proudly, shaking his antennae. "And not the kind from the movies. This is what they really look like. A friend of mine got abducted by them! And he said . . ."

Wishbone spotted Melina and Marcus sliding down the fire pole. A moment later, Travis followed them. Then he walked to the front of the store and clapped his hands. "Ladies and gentlemen," he announced, "boys and ghouls, maidens and monsters, are you ready for the Oakdale Sports and Games first annual scavenger hunt?"

All the kids cheered and clapped. *Everyone except Damont, that is,* Wishbone noticed.

"Now, this is no ordinary scavenger hunt,"

Travis continued. "On this particular search, you'll have to be quick-witted, as well as quick-footed."

Wishbone glanced up at David, Sam, and Joe. *I'd say among the four of us, our team has those bases covered.*

"Okay, here are the rules," Travis said. "There are four teams. Each team will receive one of these and one of these."

Wishbone leaped up into the air, trying to peek through the costumed crowd in front of him. "What is it? I can't see! One of *what,* and one of *what?*"

What a time to be short. Frustrated, Wish-

bone raced through the legs of the crowd so that he was able to find out what Travis was holding. *Hmm . . . a miniature jack-o'-lantern and an envelope. Got it.* His curiosity satisfied, Wishbone trotted back to his friends.

"In each of these are clues that will lead you to your first challenge," Travis explained. "Once there, you must solve a puzzle to move ahead. Your chances to advance will get tougher with each challenge. Finally, when only two teams remain, they will go on to take the most chilling challenge of all! And the prize . . . ?" Travis paused and grinned at the crowd. "A one-hundred-dollar gift certificate to shop at Oakdale Sports and Games!"

All the kids cheered again. Damont just crossed his arms over his chest and looked bored.

You don't fool me for even one second, Damont, Wishbone thought. *You're interested, just like everyone else.*

"Not everyone can win the grand prize," Travis added. "But don't worry. There will be plenty of smaller prizes. Now, if the team captains will raise their hands, we'll pass out the first clue."

Sam raised her hand. So did Jimmy.

Damont pushed Jimmy's back down, then raised his own hand. The store employees moved through the crowd, passing out the clues. Soon, each team captain held a small plastic pumpkin and an envelope. Wishbone could feel the excitement growing.

"Now, good luck—and be careful." Travis grinned. "You never know what kind of ghoulish surprises you'll find on a night like this."

"Don't remind me," Joe said quietly—so quietly that Wishbone was sure he was the only one who had heard him.

"Ready?" Travis said to everyone who had gathered around. "Open your clues!"

All around Wishbone, teams grouped next to their captains, reading the clues. Everyone except Damont. He walked up to Joe. "You feel lucky?" he asked, his face inches from Joe's. "Don't be surprised when I win that gift certificate."

Wow! I can feel the tension right down to my whiskers. Such competition, Wishbone observed. *There are four teams, but there is only one grand prize.*

Ichabod Crane is seeking a prize, as

well—Katrina Van Tassel. However, he is not alone in his goal. Every young man in the valley wants to impress her. Only time will tell if the signs will point to Ichabod as the lucky winner. . . .

Chapter Six

"Excuse me. Pardon me. Coming through."
Ichabod darted in and out of the legs of
the long row of gentlemen lined up on the
Van Tassels' wide front lawn. He could see Katrina
sitting on a bench on the front porch. She
was surrounded by her suitors, the young
men eager to date and marry her. All held
bouquets of flowers, hoping to be the lucky
man.

*So what if there are more men waiting to see
Katrina than there are in all of Sleepy Hollow?*
Ichabod thought. *It is only I who can possibly win
her heart. Who among them could instruct her in
the supernatural and share scary tales? Who among
them had dinner with the Van Tassel family two
evenings right in a row? Not to mention our love of*

singing. Ichabod had begun Katrina's singing classes after dinner the day before.

Ichabod burst into a few notes of the song he had been teaching Katrina. A flock of crows cawed loudly and took flight.

Ichabod edged forward.

"Hey!" one young man exclaimed. "Go to the back of the line. I was here first."

Ichabod pushed his hat up. "Oh, I'm sorry, dear boy. Would you like me to tell Katrina that she cannot have her singing lesson today? She'll be most disappointed."

The man looked down at Ichabod, his eyes narrowing in suspicion. "Singing lesson?" he said.

"Singing lesson," Ichabod repeated firmly. And to make his point clear, he performed a couple of howling verses he was currently teaching Katrina. Birds flapped their wings and took off from the nearby elm tree. *There they go again,* Ichabod noticed. *What is it with the birds around here?*

"Well, okay," the young man said with some hesitation. He stood aside to allow Ichabod through.

I am so clever, Ichabod thought, *sometimes I even impress myself.*

"Hello, Katrina," Ichabod called, trotting up the steps to the porch. The young man sitting beside her glared at him, but Ichabod paid no attention to him. "I'm terribly sorry to interrupt, but it is time for your singing lesson."

"Oh, of course," Katrina replied. She smiled sweetly at the young man, then stood up. The sound of thundering hooves behind Ichabod made him jump. He whirled around on all four legs and watched a large, powerfully built horse racing up the lawn toward the house.

"We'll see what Brom Bones thinks about your so-called singing lesson," the young man said as he left the porch.

The rider pulled back sharply on the reins, causing the horse to rise up onto its back legs and whinny. Then it dropped its hooves again to the ground. Ichabod recognized the rider as Abraham Van Brunt.

He was a tall, broad-shouldered man, with thick, curly black hair. He was known to all by his nickname, Brom Bones. Ichabod wondered if the "Bones" referred to those that Brom had broken. Brom was always ready for a fight or contest or prank. He was also known for his skill on horseback.

A regular party animal, Ichabod thought. *But all brawn, and no brains. I truly do not understand how a ruffian such as Brom can be admired,* Ichabod thought. *We are admired equally by the folks of Sleepy Hollow. Imagine that!*

Ichabod found it surprising that Brom was asked to settle all arguments in Sleepy Hollow and the surrounding area, even though he was a well-known practical joker and prankster. *Sure,* Ichabod thought. *Who would argue with a man built like a tree?*

The moment Brom rode onto the scene, all the other suitors vanished. None of them wanted to compete with Brom for Katrina's attention. But Ichabod planted his paws firmly and stood his ground.

I have so much more to offer Katrina. I am a man of learning. And I am liked by her parents. They love my stories of the supernatural—so does Katrina. Surely even Brom will realize that he is an unsuitable suitor.

"Hello, Brom," Katrina called from the porch, her eyes twinkling.

The pitch-black horse snorted and pawed the ground. The horse's name was Daredevil. Ichabod thought the name matched the personalities of both horse and rider.

Ichabod noticed the man carried a little clump of flowers. He also noticed a slight blush appear on Katrina's face as Brom approached the porch, leaned forward on his horse, and handed her the bouquet.

"Hello, Katrina," Brom said, as he leaped down gracefully from Daredevil. "I thought I might give you the honor of my company tonight."

"That's very sweet of you," Katrina replied.

"Maybe a moonlit ride later down by the river," Brom suggested, taking a step onto the porch.

Ichabod leaped up onto a tall oak barrel. He cleared his throat. "Ahem. Excuse me," he interrupted.

Katrina and Brom both looked over at Ichabod. Katrina smiled. Brom frowned.

"Excuse me," Ichabod repeated, "but I don't think that would be very wise."

A broad grin spread across Brom's handsome face. "Well, if it isn't Ichabod Crane," he said with sarcasm. "And tell me why you think it would be so unwise." He crossed his arms over his broad chest, awaiting the response.

Ichabod sniffed. "Oh, Katrina wouldn't be safe on such a night."

"Katrina has nothing to fear," Brom said. "Not with me around to protect her!"

At that, Ichabod laughed. *What a misguided, foolish gentleman.* "*You?* Protect Katrina?" Ichabod responded. "Only a man of knowledge, not one of pure physical strength, could protect her on this magical night. Why, look at the position of the moon." He pointed to the sky.

Brom and Katrina glanced up and then looked back at Ichabod. Brom shook his head.

"And, worst of all," Ichabod continued, amazed that he even had to point out such obvious facts, "you offer her a bouquet of foxglove, a gift bound to bring bad luck."

Hearing this, Katrina let out a cry and dropped the flowers, as if they had bitten her.

"But—" Brom started to protest, but Ichabod interrupted him.

"And after *that* unfortunate gift, you want to take her for a ride—on a *black* horse?" He shook his head so hard that his ears flapped.

"Now, see here—" Brom cried.

"A *black* horse?" Ichabod repeated. "Tonight? Why, it would seem as if you have no concern for her safety at all!"

Katrina stared openmouthed at Brom, who shrugged.

"You are probably bringing her bad luck just by standing on her property," Ichabod said boldly. *In other words,* he added silently, *vamoose! Scram! Make like a banana and split!*

Brom stood gazing at them, trying to decide what to do. So Ichabod decided for them all.

"Come along, Katrina," the love-bitten schoolmaster said. "Let us begin your singing lesson. And we will try to find some charms and remedies to get rid of all the bad omens that this big brute may have already set in motion."

Katrina nodded and hurried into the house. Ichabod gave Brom one last glaring look of warning. For a moment, Brom stared at Ichabod, stunned by the conversation that had just taken place. Then he stormed away from the porch and got back up on Daredevil. With a furious *yah!*, Brom galloped away.

Ichabod watched the horse and rider race away into the darkness. The pitch-black horse disappeared quickly into the night.

I just hope he took all of his bad luck with him! Ichabod thought. *Although I'm taking quite a chance by being here after dark.*

Ichabod sang a few notes in preparation for Katrina's singing lesson. Once again, birds fluttered out of the trees, squawking and cawing. *Perhaps Brom's ill-chosen flowers have upset the poor creatures. Well, I shall consult Cotton Mather on reversing the power of the bad luck foxgloves bring.*

With one last glance into the night, Ichabod shivered, turned, and, tail wagging, hurried into the Van Tassel farmhouse.

Things are definitely looking up for Ichabod. Perhaps all of his good-luck charms are working.

We're still waiting to see what happens with Joe's luck.

Chapter Seven

"Wow!" Wishbone exclaimed, his head whipping back and forth. "What a wacky-looking bunch of people!" Everywhere that the terrier looked, ghosts, witches, a television set, pumpkins, and pirates strolled the dark streets outside the sporting-goods store. *A television set?*

"I don't know. I'd better keep an eye on things." He leaped up onto a bench, located outside of Oakdale Sports & Games, where his friends sat puzzling over their first clue in the scavenger hunt.

Sam pulled a flashlight out of her pocket and then reopened the envelope. David and Joe leaned in close to her.

"Could you read that again?" David asked, squinting through his bright green glasses.

Sam grinned and removed David's glasses. "Uh . . . thanks," he said. "Much better."

"Yeah, Sam, what's the first clue?" Wishbone asked.

Sam aimed the flashlight so she could read the clue written on a sheet of *Oakdale Chronicle* stationery. "'When a wand is transposed and Gil has more, the Gypsy Gallery will be easy to find. If you follow the flamingos to a deafening roar, you won't be left behind.'" She shook her head and looked at Joe and David.

The friends sat silently for a moment.

"Let's think this through," David said.

"What about the pumpkin that Mr. Del Rio has given to each team captain?" Joe suggested.

Sam handed Joe the pumpkin. When he opened it, a puzzled expression crossed his face. He held it out for the others to see what was inside. "Three corks?" he said.

David leaned over Sam's shoulder to read the clue again. "What does *transposed* mean?" he asked.

"It's when two things switch places," Sam explained.

A monster with a gooey, gaping wound headed toward them. "Whoa!" Wishbone exclaimed. "I hope that's only a mask!"

But his friends were so involved with the clue that they didn't pay any attention.

"Who is Gil?" Joe asked.

"Gil Brady?" Sam suggested. "In the fifth grade?"

Joe shook his head. "I don't think so."

Sam leaned against the back of the bench and let out a sigh. "And what does *The Oakdale Chronicle* have to do with it?"

Wishbone wagged his tail. "Oh, Joe! Joe! Look! A clown!" Joe didn't answer. *These guys are completely focused on figuring out the first clue. Maybe they need my help.*

"Wait!" David cried. "Look at the words." He pointed at the words on the note. "'When a wand is transposed.' A. Wand. Wand. A."

"Wanda!" Sam exclaimed.

"'When Gil has more,'" David continued, nodding his head.

"Gilmore! Wanda Gilmore!" Joe said with a sense of excitement.

Wishbone's ears pricked up at the mention of the Talbots' next-door neighbor. Feeling his friends' excitement as they solved the puzzle, he stood and barked encouragingly.

"Wanda owns *The Oakdale Chronicle*," Sam pointed out.

"Flamingos!" all three said together.

"Let's go!" Sam announced. All three stood and headed toward Wanda's house.

Wishbone ran after them. "Hey! Not without me!" he barked.

Wishbone and his friends quickly made their way through the dark Oakdale streets. Everywhere Wishbone looked, strange new sights popped into view—people dressed as skeletons and as bats, as princesses and as trolls. But he was even more surprised by the sight awaiting him at Wanda's house.

"Will you look at that!" Wishbone stared at Wanda's house. Black plastic was wrapped around everything except the steps leading up to her porch. Cobwebs hung from the roof, and a banner of tiny ghosts fluttered in the breeze along the edge of the roof.

Wanda herself sat behind a table on the porch, with a group of children waiting in line in front of the table. She was dressed in a Gypsy outfit, with long, dangling earrings, and a towering silver turban on her head.

"Welcome to the house of Wanda," she said to a girl dressed as a giant pumpkin.

Well, Wanda will be Wanda, Wishbone thought, as he watched her go into her fortune-telling routine. *What kind of accent is that? Well, whatever it is, it sounds nice and mysterious.*

"Wonder what the future holds?" Wanda said. "Well, you have certainly come to the right place! Let's fire up the crystal ball."

Wishbone cocked his head to watch. Wanda shut her eyes and waved her hands over the large crystal ball on the table in front of her. *Nah! I don't think this odd behavior comes as a surprise to anybody,* Wishbone thought. *In fact, I'd say she was in her element.*

"Vrooom! Vroom! Vroom!" she said, like a car engine revving up.

Okay, crystal ball, prepare for take-off! Wishbone watched Wanda and the crystal ball carefully. *Ready, set . . . predict!*

"You are going to be very successful gathering candy tonight," Wanda predicted. "Show me your palm."

The trick-or-treater held out her hand, and Wanda dropped candy into it. "And your luck begins now!"

The pumpkin giggled, then dashed away. The next child in line moved into her spot on the other side of Wanda's table.

"So, do we have time to get our fortunes told?" Sam asked with a grin.

"Maybe *I* should," Joe said. Then he shook his head. "Then again, maybe I'm better off not knowing."

"Hey, look!" David cried. "The flamingos!"

Wishbone trotted over to the row of pink-plastic flamingos that lined a path around the side of Wanda's house. "So, has Wanda told your fortunes yet?" he asked the fake birds. "Any chance of flying south this year?"

Then Wishbone saw Joe, David, and Sam hurrying to the back of the house.

"Hey! Wait up!" He ran after them.

Damont Jones pushed aside the bushes and stepped into the shadows of one of the large trees lining Wanda's yard. He watched Sam, David, Joe, and Wishbone go around the side of Wanda's house.

Brilliant plan! Damont congratulated himself. *Following Sam's group. Now we'll see who is going to win that gift certificate.* He pushed his hat back on his head. "This is going to be easier than I thought," he murmured. *Let them figure out the riddles. All I want is the big prize.*

Jimmy crawled out from behind the bush where he'd been hiding. He headed toward the porch, where Wanda was sitting.

"What are you doing?" Damont demanded.

"I want to have my fortune told. I want to find out if I'm going to get an A on my report, and if we're going to win the scavenger hunt, and if I'll ever get to the moon and—"

"Jimmy!" Damont cut off his cousin's next words. He shook his head. "We don't have time for kid stuff like fortune-telling, okay? Come on. And be quiet."

Jimmy covered his mouth with his hands and nodded. Damont rolled his eyes. Then they sneaked around to the back of the house, making sure they stayed where it was pitch-dark.

We don't want Talbot and his pals to know we're on their tail. After all, Damont thought, *they need to figure out each clue for us first!*

When Wishbone caught up with his friends, Joe, David, and Sam stood staring at the entrance to Wanda's back door. Like the front of the house, everything was draped in black plastic and cobwebs. The only light came from two grinning jack-o'-lanterns. Eerie shadows danced in the dim surroundings.

"I'm detecting a definite decorating pattern here," Wishbone commented.

"'Gypsy Gallery'!" Sam read from a sign hanging over the entrance. "We were right. This is the place." She and David stepped toward the door. When Joe didn't follow them, Sam turned around. "Come on, Joe."

"I'll just wait outside," he said, handing the pumpkin with the corks in it to David.

Wishbone sat beside Joe. "Me, too. I've been in Wanda's house before."

"You're not scared, are you?" Sam asked Joe.

"It's okay, Joe," David said reassuringly. "You don't have to come."

Sam shook her head. "No," she insisted. "We do this together. We're a team!"

"I would just bring you bad luck," Joe replied.

"Come on!" Sam grabbed Joe's arm and pulled him into the Gypsy Gallery. "You, too, Wishbone," she called over her shoulder.

Wishbone glanced around, then trotted after his friends. "Well, okay, but if Wanda shows up, this was all your idea, right? She's not always thrilled to see me in her house."

"Cool!" David exclaimed as soon as they entered. "It's an old carnival shooting-gallery game!"

"Lemme see! Lemme see!" Wishbone ran forward. A few feet away from a table with a rifle on it stood a stage with a painted outdoor back-drop, complete with trees, rocks, a stream, and a bright blue sky.

Sam stepped forward and pushed a large red button on the side of the game. Carnival music started to play, and the tin animal cutouts began to move in front of the painted scenery.

"Look at the fox chasing the rabbit!" Joe said.

"Check out that tiger!" Sam exclaimed.

"And the bear!" David added.

"Wild beasts? In Wanda's house?" Wishbone leaped up to get a better view of the game. "Oh . . . they're made out of metal. Right. I knew that."

"This is great!" Sam said, as she watched the animals move back and forth.

"Hey! Look!" Joe said, pointing to the side of the machine.

Wishbone glanced up. "Yeah. A big plastic tube with little pumpkins in it. And this is important because . . . ?"

"All four of the pumpkins are still there," Sam said. "That means we're the first team here. So we're the first team to get the second clue."

That means we're ahead of Damont, Wishbone realized.

David examined the plastic tubing and the shooting-gallery game. "It looks like one of the pumpkins drops down when you hit the right target."

"That's what the corks are for!" Joe fished them out of his pocket. He studied the animals popping in and out of the scenery. "But how do we know which is the right target to aim for? We have only three shots."

"The answer must be in the clue." Sam pulled the clue out of her pocket as David and Joe gathered around her. "'If you follow the flamingos to a deafening roar, you won't be left behind,'" she read.

"We followed the flamingos, but what do we shoot?" David wondered.

"'Deafening roar,'" Joe repeated. He gazed at the animals moving back and forth, in and out of the bushes and rocks. He pointed at the tin cutout. "Try the tiger."

Sam picked up the rifle and stepped up to the machine. Joe handed her a cork and she loaded the gun. Then, steadying it against her shoulder, she took careful aim.

Clink!

"And it's a hit on the very first shot!" Wishbone announced, as the tin tiger dropped down.

"Great, Sam!" Joe cheered.

Sam blushed as she smiled. "It was a lucky shot," she said.

"Uh . . . guys," David said. "It wasn't so lucky. Nothing happened. No pumpkin dropped."

They all stared at the game. "I don't get it," Sam said, her brow wrinkling in confusion.

"It must have been the wrong target," Joe realized. He tugged the brim of his hat, staring at the animals. "So which is it?"

David peered at the shooting-gallery game. "Wait! Look!" he cried. "Over in the corner—a lion!"

"Lions roar, too," Joe said. "Just like tigers! That *has* to be the right target!"

"Got it." Sam loaded the gun again, aimed, and squeezed the trigger.

"Oooh, tough break," Wishbone said.

"Missed," Joe said. "And you've got only one more shot."

"I know." Sam took the remaining cork from Joe.

"Careful, Sam," David said. "You have to time it just right. You've got to get it before it slides behind that rock."

Sam nodded. Then she took a deep breath and aimed the gun one more time. All eyes were glued to the stage, watching the animals moving in and out of the scenery. The only sound was the cheerful carnival music. David, Joe, and Wishbone all held their breath, waiting for Sam to shoot. She squeezed the trigger.

Clink! Ding! Ding! Ding!

"You did it!" Joe cried, as the little pumpkin dropped down the plastic tube.

Wishbone leaped to his feet and twirled in the air. "Great shot, Sam!" he cheered, his tail wagging. "I never doubted you for a minute!"

"Nice shooting," a voice sneered from the doorway.

"Damont," Wishbone groaned.

Damont and Jimmy stepped into the Gypsy Gallery. "Thanks for solving the riddle for me," Damont said.

David, Joe, and Sam filed out, Wishbone leading the way. "Cheating takes all the fun out of the game, Damont," Sam said.

"Yeah, well, I'll have plenty of fun with that gift certificate," Damont replied.

"Yeah," Jimmy repeated, "we'll have plenty of fun with that gift—"

Damont cut him off. "Jimmy!"

Outside, Wishbone's sharp senses went into action. His whiskers twinged and his muscles tensed. "Cat alert!" He glanced around and spotted the black cat he had seen earlier. "That's it!" he said. "No cat crosses my territory three times in one day!"

The cat charged off, and Wishbone bounded after it. Behind him he heard Damont's voice.

"I think your luck just ran out, Talbot."

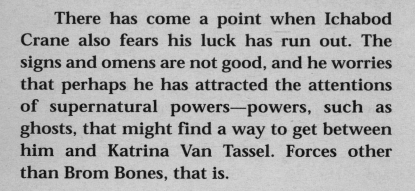

There has come a point when Ichabod Crane also fears his luck has run out. The signs and omens are not good, and he worries that perhaps he has attracted the attentions of supernatural powers—powers, such as ghosts, that might find a way to get between him and Katrina Van Tassel. Forces other than Brom Bones, that is.

Chapter Eight

Ichabod trotted alongside Katrina. He carried an empty picnic basket in his teeth. They had spent another lovely afternoon together. This time they had shared a picnic basket by the brook. Now the schoolteacher and Katrina were on their way back to the Van Tassel farm.

I could go for a few more bites of that delicious apple pie Mrs. Van Tassel provided for our picnic, he thought. *Perhaps she still has some left over from lunch.*

"Why, look," Katrina said. "I believe that is Brom Bones on Daredevil."

Ichabod glanced up and saw the huge black horse heading their way. He released the basket from his teeth, setting it on the ground, and watched Brom approach.

"Hello, Katrina," Brom called as he pulled his horse to a stop.

"Hello, Brom," she responded with a smile.

"Good day to you," Ichabod said to Brom.

Brom glanced down, first at Ichabod, then at the basket. "Have you been on a picnic?" he asked.

"Yes. It was wonderful!" Ichabod licked his chops, remembering the delicious lunch. "Katrina's mother thoughtfully provided us with several roast chickens, quite a bit of potato salad, a large roast of beef, and slices of a wonderful apple pie."

"Quite a feast," Brom commented dryly.

"Mrs. Van Tassel is always most kind to me," Ichabod explained.

"Well, Katrina, perhaps you will spend the rest of the afternoon with *me.*" Brom gazed down at Katrina. His brown eyes twinkled as he grinned at her.

A small frown clouded Katrina's features. "Brom, you should have asked me sooner," she complained. "I have already made plans for the rest of the day."

Ichabod stood tall on his four legs and faced Brom directly. "Katrina and I will be helping her mother witch-proof the house. It could take us many, many, *many* hours," he added. "So, you see, Katrina will be unable to spend any time with you at all today."

"B-b-but—" Brom sputtered.

"In fact," Ichabod continued, turning to Katrina, "we should hurry. We don't want to keep your mother waiting. Good day, Brom." He picked the basket up in his teeth, and, tail held high, he started to walk toward the farm.

"Good-bye, Brom," Katrina called, as she joined Ichabod on the path.

With a scowl, Brom turned Daredevil and galloped away.

Several times later that afternoon, Ichabod

noticed Brom riding past the Van Tassel farm. *Why, it is almost as if he is waiting for me to leave so he can come to court Katrina.* But, since Mrs. Van Tassel had invited Ichabod to stay for dinner, his visit with Katrina lasted well into the evening.

"You see, there are so many influences and powers in the world," Ichabod told Katrina. They sat side by side on the long bench in front of the fire after dinner.

Just look at Katrina, studying Cotton Mather's book with delight, Ichabod thought, his tail wagging with pleasure. *Brom Bones could never have lent her such a book. Nor could he have entertained her with such stories.*

"So the witch cast a spell over the entire town?" Katrina asked, her eyes wide with surprise.

"Hmm . . . ? What? Oh! Yes, she most certainly did. In fact, the spell was never broken until—"

Suddenly, Ichabod's words were cut off by a loud banging on the front door of the farmhouse. It swung open, letting in a huge gust of cool autumn air and a flurry of dead leaves. Brom Bones and his friends Hans and Dieter rushed in. Katrina stood up, and Ichabod scrambled to his four feet.

"Mr. Crane," Hans said, with a glance at Brom Bones. "You must come quickly. There has been a frightful event at the schoolhouse!"

"Frightful," Dieter repeated.

"Indeed?" Ichabod said.

"Yes, Ichabod," Brom said. "We need someone of your intelligence to handle this."

Well, at last the young man has come to understand the importance of my knowledge. "What has happened?" Ichabod asked.

The men exchanged looks again. "Er . . . you must come see this mysterious event with your own eyes," Hans said.

Brom nodded. "It is too unusual to describe in words."

"Unusual," Dieter repeated.

"But— I mean . . . we were—that is, I thought . . ." Ichabod protested.

"Don't worry, Ichabod," Brom told the schoolmaster. "I'll stay here and keep Katrina company."

"I'm sure the situation can wait until morning," Ichabod said.

"Maybe you should go," Katrina said. "I know that you're the only man qualified to examine an unusual scene."

"Well, perhaps you're right, Katrina," Ichabod

said, picking up his three-cornered hat. "All right. I'll go."

He trotted over to the door as Brom sat on the bench beside Katrina.

"Well, what are we waiting for?" Ichabod demanded of Hans and Dieter. "Is this a crisis, or what?"

"I shall patrol the area around the school-house," Dieter said. He left the farmhouse, hopped on his horse, and then quickly rode off into the dark night.

Hans accompanied Ichabod to the school-house. However, every time Ichabod questioned the man about the emergency, Hans just shook his head and claimed it was too impossible to describe. "You'll just have to see for yourself," he told the puzzled schoolmaster.

"Now, then, what is so important that it could not wait until morning?" Ichabod demanded when they arrived at the schoolhouse. He sat in front of the door of the school to scratch behind his ear with his hind leg.

Instead of answering, Hans flung open the door, holding a lantern in front of him. Ichabod turned to look inside and froze in mid-scratch. He gasped at the sight of his topsy-turvy school-room!

The children's desks and benches were stacked on top of one another up to the ceiling! Their copybooks perched from shelves that no child could have reached. The dunce cap—worn by misbehaving children—sat on the leg of an upside-down table. Pencils had spelled out the word *Beware* on the floor.

Ichabod's four legs trembled with fear. "Poltergeists!" he cried. "A poltergeist has moved through here!"

"A *what?*" Hans looked blankly at Ichabod.

"A poltergeist! A ghost! A spirit that plays pranks and causes trouble." Ichabod paced the schoolroom, his nails clicking on the rough wood floor.

"You mean this mess could not have been caused by a human being?" Hans asked, waving his hands at the mess.

"Impossible," Ichabod told him. "No, this sort of disorder would only be the work of a prankster ghost." Ichabod shook his head. "I have avoided supernatural trouble since I arrived in this village—even with the huge ghost population here. But now I see that my luck has finally run out."

"My, my," Hans answered with sympathy.

"You know, I suspected something like

105

this might happen when the chimney was mysteriously stopped up a few days ago, and we were smoked out of the schoolhouse. Do you remember that?"

"Why, yes, I remember it very well," Hans replied with a smile not seen by Ichabod.

"Well, here is the final proof that a ghost was here," Ichabod continued. "Who but a mean-spirited ghost would do such a thing?"

"Who, indeed?" Hans said.

"I have a good deal of work to do here," Ichabod told Hans. "I have to clean up and straighten out my schoolroom. Then I must do all I can to protect the schoolroom in the future. So, perhaps you should go—unless you would like to help me."

"No, no, I'll leave that to the expert," Hans said. Without another word, he left the schoolhouse. Ichabod was alone.

Alone in the dark! The lantern light had gone out. Ichabod raced over to relight the lantern and raised the wick. Holding a match in his teeth, he struck it hard against the wood floor. Then he lit the wick. The lantern light cast eerie shadows all over the bewitched room.

Poor Hans, Ichabod thought, lifting the lantern in his teeth. *He must have been even more terrified than I. After all, I have some knowledge and understanding of these kinds of supernatural events.*

Ichabod placed the lantern on the floor and went to work to undo the mess created by the spirits. Each little gust of wind that caused the lantern light to flicker made him jump.

There was no way to know if the ghosts had left the area. They could be waiting outside, watching . . . laughing . . . planning their next prank! Ichabod hurried about his work. He pushed the benches into place, and he set the books on their shelves with chattering teeth.

Once the schoolroom was back in its orderly fashion, it was time to take care of the larger, more fearful problem.

I must concentrate all my energies to get rid of the ghost. Things have become quite dangerous in Sleepy Hollow.

Ichabod paced back and forth. *For some reason, I am the target of this supernatural attention. Maybe the spirits are bored and are looking for a challenge. They know that I have the knowledge that can defeat them. Oh, dear, oh, dear, oh, dear! How will I rid myself of this haunting? I shall have to check my books. I am sure Cotton Mather will have much to say on this subject.*

Ichabod nosed through the papers he

found scattered on the floor. *Could witches be holding their meetings here?* He shivered, and his fur stood on end at the thought. *If so, I'd better get out of here now!*

Ichabod ran out the schoolhouse door. He hurried home, making sure his warning bell rang loudly enough to drive away any troublesome ghosts.

Oh, my, this is an omen of terrible things to come. I'm sure of it! Oh, dear, oh, dear. What next?

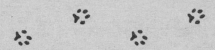

With Damont hot on their trail, Sam, Joe, and David are wondering what is waiting next for them, too. And what tricks might Damont have up his sleeve?!

Chapter Nine

Joe glanced back at the Gypsy Gallery, knowing that Damont was inside. "I can't believe he followed us," he said. "Just my luck." Then he looked around. "Wishbone?" Joe called. He turned to David and Sam. "Where do you think Wishbone went?"

David and Sam stood together, studying the second clue. David looked up and scanned the area. "Maybe Wishbone went home," he suggested.

"Can you two wait here while I go find him? I'll check my house first. Maybe my mom has seen him," Joe said.

"We don't have much time," Sam pointed out. "Damont is right behind us. If he gets to the next clue first—"

"I'm not going anywhere without Wishbone," Joe said.

Sam and David exchanged a look.

"Then we'd better find him quickly," Sam said.

Just as the three friends headed off next door to the Talbot house, Damont and Jimmy came out from the Gypsy Gallery. Damont tossed the mini-pumpkin holding the next clue up into the air. Catching it neatly, he grinned at Joe. "See you later."

Joe shook his head, then hurried to his house. Sam and David followed and then sat down outside while Joe walked in, searching for Wishbone. He came back out onto the front steps.

"Was he in there?" David asked, getting to his feet.

"No," Joe reported. Then he sighed. "I *knew* I should have stayed home tonight."

"Now what are we going to do?" David asked.

Sam looked at Joe. "We're losing time," she said. "Damont's already on his way to the next clue. But, if you want to look for Wishbone, we'll help you."

"Thanks," Joe said. "But—" He stopped when he heard the sound of barking. "That's

Wishbone!" Joe exclaimed. He led his friends to the back of the house.

Wishbone had chased the cat to the alley behind his house. Now he stood on his hind legs, his front paws resting on the back fence, barking up at the black cat. "Here, kitty, kitty!" But the cat ignored him. Instead, it strolled

along the top of the narrow fence. Without even a meow, the cat leaped down the other side of the fence and disappeared out of view.

"Hey! I can't do that," Wishbone complained. "No fair!"

"Wishbone!" Joe called as he ran into the alley. Sam and David were right behind him.

"Don't you worry, Joe," Wishbone told

his pal. "I took care of him for you. Did you see that cat run? I scared him off."

Joe reached down and patted Wishbone. "Stick around, okay, buddy?"

"Where to next?" Wishbone asked.

"Great! Now we can finish!" Sam declared. "What's the next clue?"

David opened the little pumpkin and pulled out a small piece of paper. "Okay," he said. "Here it is: 'Follow Dart to the Derby, where the Thoroughbreds and mixed breeds meet. If you don't want to lose, then you must choose an enchantress light on her feet.'" He glanced at the others, a puzzled expression on his face.

Sam wrinkled her brow. "A racetrack? In Oakdale?"

"The only 'dart' I know is the Dart Animal Clinic," Joe said.

Sam's face broke into a broad grin. "That's it! 'Where the Thoroughbreds and mixed breeds meet!'"

"Let's go!" David cried.

Wishbone backed up and sat down. "Animal clinic? *Oooooh, noooo!* Not me. No way!"

"You two go on ahead," Joe said. "I'll stay here."

"Oh, come on, Joe," David urged.

Joe shook his head. "You two guys are up for this. I'm not. Besides, I should take Wishbone into the house, anyway."

"That's right, Joe." Wishbone headed for the house.

Sam placed her hands squarely on her hips. "Look, Joe," she said, "we're not splitting up our team."

"Right," David agreed. David and Sam gave each other a quick nod. Then they each grabbed one of Joe's arms and started to drag him down the alley.

"Hey!" Joe laughed. "Okay, okay. Come on, Wishbone."

"No, no, Joe," Wishbone called after them. "You are completely right. We should go into the house. We should . . ." But his friends had already turned the corner. He ran after them. "Wait up!"

Soon, they arrived at the Dart Animal Clinic. Too soon, as far as Wishbone was concerned.

Sam, Joe, and David rushed inside, but Wishbone paced back and forth on the pavement in front, giving himself a pep talk. "Okay, Wishbone," he said to himself. "You can do this.

It's just the animal clinic. Here we go." Taking a deep breath, he went into the clinic.

And then he instantly ran out.

"Oooh, my stomach," he moaned.

"Wishbone?" Joe called from inside.

"Okay, do it for Joe," Wishbone told himself. "Do it for Joe."

"Come on, Wishbone—over here," he heard Joe say.

"I hope you appreciate this, Joe," he told his friend as he trotted back inside. "I'm only in here because you need me. But I'm telling you—if I see one needle, I am outta here!"

Joe, Sam, and David gathered around an antique horse-race game. They gazed down at a racetrack with a brightly painted finish line. Little metal horses were mounted on sticks that would move along the grooves in the metal track.

"Are you ready?" David asked.

"Yes!" Sam said eagerly.

"Let's get this over with," Wishbone gasped. "I can't breathe in here." He crawled along the floor and flopped down.

David pushed a bright red button and the game came to life. A trumpet blasted from tiny loudspeakers, signaling the start of the race.

Then the trumpet sound died out and lights began to flash on the backboard. The words *Derby Daze* were written across the top, and the horses' names were listed below.

"Guys, look." Sam pointed to the side of the antique game where another plastic tube with pumpkins in it was attached.

"Only three pumpkins left," David said.

"That means Damont is ahead of us," Sam said. "We have to catch up!"

Wishbone leaped up and down, trying to get a glimpse of the toy racetrack. "What is it? What's happening?"

A crackling sound startled them. "Welcome to the Derby Daze," a voice blared from the loudspeakers. "Today's horses are Galloping Goblin, Flying Sorceress, Witch's Broomstick, and Glue Factory. You have thirty seconds to choose the winning horse."

"We have to pick a horse!" Sam exclaimed. She pointed at the levers by the horses' names. "Quick! Read the clue again."

David reread the clue. "'If you don't want to lose, then you must choose an enchantress light on her feet.'" He studied the names of the horses lit up on the machine. "Enchantress," he murmured, thinking it over. Then he bright-

ened. "Witch! It must be Witch's Broomstick."
He reached for the lever.

"No—wait!" Joe stopped him. "Read the last
part again."

"You now have fifteen seconds to choose
the winning horse," the game announced.

"Don't interrupt," Wishbone told the
machine. "You're making it hard to think!"

"'. . . Choose an enchantress light on her
feet,'" David repeated. "See? Light on her feet.
Witches fly on broomsticks."

Joe studied the clue. "No. It says to pick the
enchantress, not her broom."

"Flying Sorceress!" Sam suggested.

"Could someone please pick me up so I can
see!" Wishbone jumped up to try to see what
was happening.

The machine continued its countdown.
"You must choose the winning horse in five,
four, three, two—"

Sam reached out and pushed the lever for
Flying Sorceress—and the race began.

"And they're off!" the game announced.

Sam, David, and Joe leaned in over the
machine, cheering on their horse.

"Let's go! Come on!" Sam shouted.

"Faster! Faster!" David chanted.

"Go, Sorceress! Go!" Joe yelled.

Wishbone jumped up and down behind them. "Who's winning? Who's winning? Guys!"

The three kids kept their eyes on the game as they whooped and cheered.

Wishbone leaped into the air and twirled. *I don't know what's going on, but it sure sounds like fun!* He twirled again. "Wa-hoo! Yippee! Go, team!"

"And the winner is . . . Flying Sorceress!" the announcement blared from the loudspeakers.

"We won!" Sam cried. A jack-o'-lantern dropped down the plastic chute into the tray.

"All right! We won! So . . . what did we win?" Wishbone trotted over and sniffed the pumpkin David held in his hand. "What? No food?"

"What does it say?" Sam asked.

David opened up the pumpkin and pulled out the clue. "It says, 'Every year when the leaves are green, Jackson's Carnival can be seen. Purple, red, yellow, and blue, which of these would you pursue?'"

Wishbone sat back and scratched under his chin with his hind leg. "Oh, that's easy."

"Jackson's Carnival?" David glanced at Joe and Sam.

Sam took the pumpkin from David. She held it upside down and shook it. A little round coin dropped into her palm. "Oh, look," she said, holding it up. "A token."

"But where do we go?" Joe wondered.

David glanced down at the note again. "'Every year when the leaves are green'?"

"Does that mean the summer carnival?" Sam guessed.

Joe snapped his fingers. "In Jackson Park!" he exclaimed.

"Good one, Joe!" Wishbone wagged his tail as he followed Joe, Sam, and David out of the animal clinic.

"Oooooh, creepy," Wishbone said as he watched a flashlight beam flicker over the quiet park. Sam, David, and Joe carefully walked among the trees until they came to a clearing. Sam's flashlight threw light on a circus tent. Jack-o'-lanterns sat on top of two poles standing beside the tent entrance.

"Of course!" Sam exclaimed to the boys. "This is where the summer carnival is always set up. Come on!"

They walked through the tent flap and David gasped. "Whoa! This is really incredible!" he exclaimed.

"What is it?" Wishbone raced through David's legs and stared at the enormous glass case sitting in the center of the tent. "Will you look at that—whatever it is."

Inside the case was a complicated game filled with levers, slides, toys, dominoes, mobiles, and things Wishbone couldn't identify. Everything seemed to be hooked up to everything else. At the top were six color-coded coin slots. Like all the other games, this contraption also had a plastic tube attached to the side.

Sam pointed to the tube. "There are still three pumpkins left!" she said.

"We're still in the game," Joe said.

"But Damont is one step ahead of us," Sam warned. "At least we're ahead of the other two teams. We need to figure this out—and fast!"

David walked all around the huge mechanical setup. "This is awesome," he murmured. Fascinated by the device, David looked as if he was in his own world.

Then Wishbone lay down to watch David examine the game. "Uh-oh. We lost David," he observed.

Joe looked up at the top of the machine. "Which slot?" he asked, holding up the coin from the pumpkin clue.

"We have to choose a color," Sam said. She reread the clue. "'Purple, red, yellow, and blue.'" She glanced back up at the slots. "Well, there are six slots, and the clue asks which of the four colors I just mentioned would we pursue. That narrows it down to four."

Wishbone watched David. "I've got to get one of these," David said.

"Oh, yeah, we really lost him," Wishbone said.

Sam and Joe exchanged an amused look. "Uh . . . David," Sam said, "we could use your help here."

"Yes," Joe added. "Which color slot do we put the coin in?"

"It's the orange one," David said, his eyes never leaving the game.

"What?" Sam's eyebrows rose with surprise.

"That was quick," Wishbone said.

"How did you figure that out?" Joe asked.

David finally looked away from the big contraption. "It's the only color on the machine that's not mentioned anywhere in the clue," he explained.

Sam glanced down at the clue. "He's right! It says the leaves are green. Then it lists the other colors. No orange!" She approached the color slots, with the coin raised.

"Wait!" David called. Sam stopped in her tracks and turned to face David. He hurried over to her. "Let me do it."

"Sure." She handed him the coin with a grin. "Be my guest."

David slipped the coin into the orange slot. Instantly, the machine went into action. A marble rolled down a spiral ramp into a funnel, which made a pulley lift a lever, ringing a bell.

"Whoa!" Wishbone exclaimed. "Is Halloween always so noisy?"

The rolling marble kept triggering off more and more surprises: A tiny hammer knocked over a domino, sending the rest tumbling in a straight line. The last domino then hit a miniature bucket, which lifted the marble to a different level. The game was in constant motion. Wishbone rested his paws on the side of the glass, trying to keep track of where the marble was going. Up, down, around, in, out, over, under. The marble rolled down another ramp, causing a tiny boxing glove to hit another bell. *Ding!*

"This is making me really dizzy!" Wishbone said.

Finally, a bucket dropped a toy bone into a little dog-food bowl that sat in front of a dog house. A stuffed dog reached out its neck from inside the dog house, then snatched up the bone in its mouth. The moment it returned to the dog house, the last pumpkin dropped down the chute.

"That was really kind of cool," Wishbone remarked.

Joe grabbed the pumpkin and opened it. "A marble?" he said, holding up the little round green stone. Then he pulled out a small piece of paper and stared down at it.

"Ooh! Ooh! Let me see!" Wishbone trotted over to the others.

"Uh-oh. This can't be happening," Joe murmured. He glanced at Sam and David, a worried expression on his face.

"What is it, Joe?" Wishbone asked. "What does it say?"

Joe gulped and read the clue aloud: "'You are invited to a Tea Party at Thirteen Thunder Road. . . .'"

Joe looked at his friends for a moment. They were all silent.

"Thunder Road . . ." Joe repeated in a low whisper.

Cool! A party! I love parties. . . . But I have a funny feeling this party is going to be a little bit different from any other one I've ever been to. Halloween seems to have that effect on everything.

Ichabod is also excited about receiving a party invitation—to a Halloween party at the Van Tassel farm!

Chapter Ten

Ichabod sat on his desk in the schoolhouse. He looked down at the delightful card. His tail wagged with excitement. A servant from the Van Tassel farm had just delivered the Halloween party invitation.

"Oh, thank you," Ichabod told the young servant. "Please tell the Van Tassels I shall be most honored to attend their All Hallow's Eve party tonight!"

With a quick nod, the servant left the schoolhouse, just as the children began to arrive for class.

"Hello! Hello! Hello!" Ichabod greeted the students with enthusiasm. "Isn't it a glorious day!"

"It is, Mr. Crane," Andrew replied. "I wish

we could spend it outside playing hoops or hop-scotch."

"Perhaps you shall be able to get a game in," Ichabod told the boy.

I know just what Andrew means, he thought. *I could go for a game myself. I feel as lighthearted as a pup! Oooh, I love parties! All that fun! All that food! And the sooner I get through today's lessons, the sooner I will get to the party.*

"Now, children, no dilly-dallying!" Ichabod said. "We must get to our lessons right away! Please take out your copybooks and write down these arithmetic problems."

As the class wrote in their books, two more children hurried in through the doorway. Ichabod pointed to their places on the benches. Then he continued to recite the arithmetic problems. *No sense in wasting time scolding the latecomers,* he thought. *I don't wish to bring even a bit of unpleasantness to such a wonderful day.*

After giving the class a few brief minutes to work out the arithmetic problems, Ichabod instructed them to stop and put away their copybooks. "We'll check the answers next week!" he told the class.

A few of the children murmured to one another in surprise.

"Well, you are all such excellent students, I'm sure your answers are correct!" he added. "Now, on to our history lesson!"

Ichabod nosed open a large book. A ribbon marked the spot where he had left off the previous day.

"Now, let me see. . . ." He looked at his lesson plan on the desk, then back at the book. "It seems that we were going to discuss the rise and fall of the Roman Empire."

That could take all morning, he realized. *And we still have reciting, spelling, and important dates in the birth of our nation to get through.*

Ichabod sat up on his haunches and spoke to the class. "Okay, everyone, here's the short version. The Roman Empire rose and then it fell. An update at eleven—eleven A.M.—next week, that is. Okay, what's next?"

Ichabod gazed out at the roomful of children.

"I know!" he said. "Instead of having our usual form of recitation, let's make it a game. We'll see how quickly we can recite these lines. On the count of three. Ready? One . . . two . . . three! Open your reading books!"

The children giggled and flipped their books open on their desks.

"I will tap a rhythm for you to recite to,"

Ichabod said. "On your mark . . . get set . . . *read!*"

The first child Ichabod pointed to stood and recited the line from the book. At the same time, Ichabod beat a rhythm on his desk with his paws. Then the next child popped up and recited the following line. Each child tried to outdo the speed of the child who spoke before. Ichabod tapped faster and louder as the children read line after line of their lesson. By the time the very last child jumped up and shouted out the final words, they were all gasping and out of breath.

"Oh, well done!" Ichabod cried.

"That was fun!" Andrew exclaimed. "Let's do it again!"

"We'll use the same system with our multiplication tables," Ichabod suggested, his tail wagging with delight.

The children nodded eagerly. Ichabod pounded an even faster rhythm.

"Two times two is four!" the first child chanted.

Before he sat down, the second child leaped to her feet. "Four times four is sixteen!" she cried.

And so they went through the whole class,

laughing and calling out the answers as fast as they could.

On to important dates in our nation's birth, Ichabod thought. *We're in the home stretch now.*

Children giving the wrong answers were simply told that they would do better the next time. Those providing correct responses were congratulated with such cheer that Ichabod's barks could be heard echoing in the valleys for miles around.

"And in what year did Christopher Columbus come to America?" Ichabod asked Peter. *This is the final question of the day,* Ichabod decided. *Come on, Peter. We're on a roll here. We're counting on you.*

Peter looked worried. "The year?" he asked, looking confused.

Ichabod nodded. "Yes, Peter—the year."

"The year," Peter repeated. "The year . . ." His face brightened. "I know! Fourteen hundred and . . . fourteen hundred and . . . fourteen hundred and . . ." Peter's expression clouded over.

"That's right!" Ichabod exclaimed, leaping so high that all four feet left his chair.

"But I didn't finish my answer!" Peter said.

"Oh, but I could see that 1492 was right on

the tip of your tongue. And with that," Ichabod added, "class is dismissed!"

All of the children stared at Ichabod for a moment, frozen in shock.

"Go on!" Ichabod urged. "The school day is over. Make tracks!"

"Hooray!" several children cried. The students leaped off their benches, whooping and cheering. Ichabod gleefully shouted louder than the rest. Books were flung aside without being put away on the shelves. Inkstands were overturned and benches tipped over. Everyone burst out of the schoolhouse, thrilled to be released so early in the day.

Especially me! Ichabod thought. "See you all next week," Ichabod called to the children as he trotted away from the schoolhouse. He charged past Raven Rock. "See you later, Shrieking Woman in White," he said, remembering the story of the weeping ghost.

Hmm . . . he thought. *Perhaps I shouldn't have put it quite that way. Oh, well, no matter. Nothing will frighten me today! Not even ghosts!*

He hurried home toward the Van Ripper farm. *I hope Mr. Van Ripper doesn't have too many chores lined up for me,* Ichabod thought. Ichabod always helped with the farmwork wherever he

stayed each new week. Mr. Van Ripper never failed to find tasks for Ichabod to do.

Let's see. . . . Storing the hay is done, but on a farm there is always a fence to mend, livestock to tend, and wood to cut for the fire.

Ichabod picked up speed. *Well, even if Mr. Van Ripper does have chores in mind for me, getting out of school early leaves me plenty of time to prepare for the party!*

Ichabod trotted over the bumpy road.

I shall see my sweet Katrina! I shall spend a whole evening of merriment with her, with all the village to see what a good couple we make. He leaped over a small shrub and ducked under a low tree branch without skipping a beat.

Perhaps I should arrive early and help Mrs. Van Tassel set out the food. I wouldn't mind sampling a few morsels—simply for tasting purposes, of course! I'm sure Mrs. Van Tassel would want to be sure that every bite is perfect for her guests. Ichabod couldn't resist—he jumped into a deep pile of leaves, laughing as they flew into the air. *Food-testing! It's a tough job, but somebody has to do it!*

Ichabod arrived at the Van Ripper farmhouse in record time. His mind was filled with ideas for all the games he and Katrina might play, and the wonderful stories he could tell her.

Let's see, perhaps I can introduce the idea of charades. She should enjoy that! Or—I know!—we could play blind man's bluff! Ichabod's tail wagged quickly with anticipation for the party ahead.

Back in his tiny, temporary room, Ichabod brushed his fur until it gleamed. He checked himself in the mirror. *Fur—smooth and shining white. Paws—not a thorn or speck of mud.*

Satisfied, he trotted over to his closet. *Now, to select my party attire.* Ichabod looked through his wardrobe and picked out his very best short pants, vest, and cutaway coat. *Of course, picking my outfit is quite easy, since I have only two sets of short pants and vests to choose from, and a single dress coat for Sunday.*

He put on his woolen tights and the pants. He polished his anti-witch bell. Then he made sure to fasten it securely to a button on his brocade vest. Over it all he put his long, cutaway coat. His tail poked out of the split back.

Groomed and dressed, he stood in front of the mirror again, admiring his whiskers. *Looking good, Ichabod!* Then he went into his tried-and-true, never-fail "aren't I cute?" expression. *Perfect! I shall have an answer ready for every situation at the party,* he told himself.

Who knew whom he would be meeting at

the party? After all, not only was he going to be enjoying Katrina's company. He would be meeting important people from all around the county. Those people might someday play a part in his future plans. That future, if all went well, would include Katrina.

"Would you care to have this dance?" Ichabod said to his reflection in the mirror. He checked out his expression. *Perfect!* He went through a few dance steps.

"Would I care to *what?*" a voice demanded behind him.

Ichabod whirled around and blushed. *Ooops!* "You caught me," Ichabod confessed to Mr. Van Ripper. "I thought I would do a small rehearsal for the party. I just wanted to be sure I would make a good impression."

"Humph!" Mr. Van Ripper grunted.

He's a man of few words, Ichabod thought once again. He had had that thought often, ever since he came to live at Mr. Van Ripper's farm. *And he's also a man of very few pounds.* Ichabod gazed at his skinny, old, current landlord.

The aged farmer had a very long white beard, and wiry hair that matched his wiry eyebrows.

He always looks as if he's about to fly into a

rage, Ichabod observed. *I just hope he is in a good mood now so that I may ask him my favor.*

"Er . . . Mr. Van Ripper," Ichabod said. "I was wondering if perhaps you might be willing to lend me one of your fine horses tonight."

Mr. Van Ripper narrowed his eyes at Ichabod. He studied his tenant carefully, but didn't say a word.

Well, at least he didn't say no! So far, so good. Ichabod pressed on, making his point. "As you know," Ichabod continued, "the Van Tassels are citizens of the highest class, and they are well known as fine entertainers. Their party will

certainly attract excellent company." Ichabod lowered his head shyly. "I am hoping I shall be able to arrive at their farm looking like a gentleman myself. With your kind generosity, of course, I could do that."

"Humph!" Mr. Van Ripper tugged on his long beard.

Pretty please? Ichabod added silently. He sighed.

After an uncomfortable moment of silence, Mr. Van Ripper released his beard. "I have *one* horse I can lend you. I'll even throw in a saddle. But be careful with the animal. They don't grow on trees, you know!"

That was the longest speech Ichabod had ever heard Mr. Van Ripper give in one stretch.

"Oh, thank you! Thank you! I shall guard it with my life!" Hearing the words he had just said, Ichabod felt a slight shiver. Once again he wondered if what he had just said was stated in an unlucky way.

Ichabod gave himself one last approving look in the mirror. Then he trotted after Mr. Van Ripper out to the stable, his tail wagging.

"That one," Mr. Van Ripper said, pointing to a stall at the end of the row. "Gunpowder."

"What a noble and energetic name," said

Ichabod. *Perhaps this horse will give Brom's Daredevil a run for his money!*

Without another word, the old farmer turned and left the stable.

"Thank you," Ichabod called after the man. Then he walked toward the stall . . . and stopped in his tracks.

"Oh, my," he murmured. "This beast has seen better days."

Ichabod studied the thin creature. One blind eye glared unseeing at the world, milky-white and strange. The other eye flashed with a mean spark—meaner even than Mr. Van Ripper. *In fact,* Ichabod noted, *the horse and the owner seem to share many qualities.*

"He could stand some grooming." Ichabod jumped up onto an overturned tree stump that Mr. Van Ripper used to hold the stall's gate open. He reached out to brush the horse's mane. "Yikes!" he cried, as the horse snapped his yellow teeth at him. "Okay, okay, I won't mess with the hair!"

Ichabod leaped into the saddle and picked up the reins in his teeth.

"Let us go, Gunpowder!" he instructed the horse.

The old, broken-down horse let out a snort.

It flicked its tangled, scraggly tail. But it took not a single step. To Ichabod, the horse almost seemed to sneer.

Hmm . . . Where's the On button for this beast? Ichabod was so pleased about the upcoming party, however, that even a hesitant horse would not stand in his way.

"I'll make you a deal, Gunpowder," he promised the mean-tempered animal. "You let me ride you tonight, and I'll make sure you'll find some extra carrots in your food trough tomorrow." *Now, there's an offer he can't refuse.*

Ichabod was right! Slowly, and with the jerkiest stride that Ichabod had ever experienced, Gunpowder finally began to move. *Sl-o-o-o-w-w-l-y-y-y.*

"Oh, well done!" Ichabod cried. He wanted to give the horse every bit of encouragement. *This is going to be quite an unsteady ride,* he realized. He gripped the pommel on the saddle with his paws and clung tightly to the reins with his teeth. *But we are finally on our way!*

It was a long ride to the Van Tassel farm. Ichabod and Gunpowder rode past Raven Rock and the schoolhouse.

"I was just kidding about seeing The Shrieking Woman in White later," he called out, just in case any ghosts might be listening. Then he turned onto the rocky path that led into the Sleepy Hollow woods.

The pair rode through the walnut groves and over the little bridge by the church. Ichabod remembered to hold his breath to keep away bad luck as he passed by the cemetery. Shivering under his fur, he thought of the Headless Horseman's body lying in its grave.

"It looks like there's a storm brewing," he murmured to his horse. Dark storm clouds gathered overhead, and the screeching of the birds meant that bad weather was on the way. Already Ichabod could feel the wind whipping up, making his fur bristle. Ichabod's ears pricked up at the whistling in the trees and crackling leaves crunching under Gunpowder's hooves. They made for a sad combination, and Ichabod's cheerful mood began to disappear. He started to feel worried.

This is just the kind of weather meant for witches, Ichabod thought. *Or even a visit from the Headless Horseman. The signs are all here. And tonight is Halloween!*

Ichabod's horse's hooves now made wet, squishy sounds as they traveled through a marshy section of Sleepy Hollow known as

Wiley's Swamp. For a moment Ichabod wondered who Wiley was, and why he had a swamp named after him. *Could Wiley himself lie deep in the marshy ground? Is he waiting to pull unsuspecting riders under the swamp to their doom? Halloween would be the perfect night for such a thing!*

Then Ichabod had another idea. *Perhaps Wiley was a victim of the Headless Horseman! Yes, that would be quite logical. Naming the swamp for poor Wiley would be a reminder for others to beware of the feared ghost! Oh, how many lives has the Headless Horseman claimed?*

Ichabod guided Gunpowder along the wooden planks that crossed the stream and led them out of the swamp. *All Hallow's Eve,* he thought. *The night when even restful spirits rise up from their graves to roam the earth and haunt the living.* He shivered in the saddle as he continued on his way.

There it is! Ichabod spotted the Van Tassel farm and the crowds of people standing around on the wide lawn. "How about moving into second gear?" Ichabod asked Gunpowder. To his surprise and delight, the horse obeyed and picked up a little speed.

Why, half of the county must be here, Ichabod

observed. He saw groomsmen leading horses to stables and helping ladies out of coaches and carriages. People were greeting one another merrily. Ichabod's ears picked up the sound of a fiddler playing a festive tune.

The jerking, uncomfortable, and spooky ride was over. Ichabod leaped off Gunpowder. He handed over the reins to one of the Van Tassel servants. Then, tail wagging, he trotted merrily across the lawn.

Ichabod glanced up at the sound of giggling. He spotted Brom Bones sitting on the huge, pitch-black Daredevil, surrounded by a crowd of young women. He seemed to be performing tricks for the admiring group.

Well, well, well, Katrina is not among them, Ichabod noticed. *And while Brom is outside amusing these folk, he cannot also be inside entertaining Katrina.* Ichabod hurried toward the house. *Yes, this is my lucky day, after all!*

Chapter Eleven

"Welcome to our party, Ichabod!" Mr. Van Tassel, Katrina's father, greeted the schoolmaster on the front porch. The strong wind whipped Mr. Van Tassel's long hair about his face and scattered swirling leaves across the buckled shoes on his feet. Despite the chilly weather, the gentleman's smile was warm and happy.

"I am so pleased to be here," Ichabod said, his tail wagging. Already his whiskers tingled from the glorious aromas coming from the farmhouse.

Mr. Van Tassel shook his paw. "Please," he said, motioning toward the door. "Go inside and help yourself to the feast!"

"Well, if you insist . . ." Ichabod replied.

He handed his hat to a nearby servant and then trotted through the doorway. Ichabod gazed at all the delicious dishes piled high on the long wooden table. His mouth watered as he studied the platters of shortcakes, ginger cakes, and honey cakes. Then there were Mrs. Van Tassel's famous pies. Next, Ichabod spotted the hams, the smoked beef, and roast chickens. He nearly fainted, overcome by the enormous amount of food. "So much food, so little time!" he declared.

He picked up a plate and then piled it high with tasty treats. After licking his plate clean, he went back to the buffet table and piled his plate high again. And still a third time! Finally, his appetite temporarily satisfied, Ichabod lay down to watch the other partygoers.

Ichabod suddenly sat straight up on his haunches. *Katrina! Why, I was so distracted by the wonderful food that I have not yet greeted my lovely hostess.* Ichabod leaped to his four feet and hurried into the adjoining parlor, searching for Katrina.

There she is! Katrina stood in a corner, smiling and clapping in time to the music being played by a hired orchestra. Ichabod checked to be sure he had no crumbs in his whiskers. Then

he trotted over to the young woman, nails clicking on the wood floor.

"Hello, Katrina!" he said. He gazed at her with his best smile, just as he had practiced at home.

"Hello, Mr. Crane," Katrina replied. "Is it not a lovely party?"

"Oh, yes, it is, indeed!" Ichabod nodded so enthusiastically that his ears flapped up and down.

Katrina waved at two young farmers who had just entered the room. Then she smiled at Ichabod. "I see the stormy weather hasn't kept people away," Katrina said, pleased at the guest turnout.

Ichabod glanced at the window. The brewing storm caused the trees to dance wildly, scratching at the windowpanes. He shivered, remembering that Major Andre's ghost haunted those very woods behind the house. Then he looked back at Katrina.

"How could anyone stay away from a party as much fun as this?" Ichabod told Katrina. "And those musicians are quite fine!" The music was delightful, making his tail wag and his ears twitch. The rhythm was so catching that he could barely keep his four paws planted on the floor. "Would you care to dance?"

"I would love to, Mr. Crane!"

Katrina followed him onto the dance floor. Ichabod leaped up into the air and twirled, landing on his four legs, only to bound up once again. Katrina laughed gaily as she whirled around the dance floor, Ichabod at her heels. Other couples made room for the two joyful dancers. As Ichabod whirled around once more, he noticed Brom standing in the doorway, a scowl on his face.

Sorry, Brom, Ichabod thought, as his paws left the ground again. *Not everyone can be as light on their feet as I am.* Ichabod ducked and twirled. *Smooth move!* Ichabod congratulated himself on his fancy footwork. *No one could accuse me of having two left paws.*

After Ichabod and Katrina took several more turns on the dance floor, the musicians took a break. "Let's get some fresh air out on the porch," Katrina suggested. "There are people bobbing for apples there!"

"I'd love to!" Ichabod followed the young woman through the happy crowd. The front porch had been enclosed against the bad weather. People sat on the benches that lined the front wall of the house, chatting and drinking cider. A large wooden bucket sat on a table, and a man bent over it, trying to grasp an apple in his teeth. Two girls watching him laughed as he lifted his head out of the bucket, water dripping down his face.

"I give up!" the man said with a grin. One girl gave him a thick cloth so he could wipe his face. Then the other girl picked his hat up off the bench and handed it to him as the three friends reentered the main house.

"Care to bob for apples, Ichabod?" Katrina asked.

Ichabod leaped up onto the table and looked into the bucket of water. Then he looked back at Katrina. "Bobbing for apples. What a fun game. Yes, I think I will try this, actually." *After all, I have the perfect kind of teeth for a game such as this one!* "Let's see. . . ."

Ichabod placed his paws on the sides of the bucket to steady himself.

"Here I go!"

He plunged his muzzle into the water, trying to grab an apple in his sharp teeth. But his nose kept pushing the apples out of reach. He turned his head this way and that, his paws occasionally slipping into the water. Finally, he managed to nose an apple over to the side of the bucket. Opening his mouth wide, he sank his teeth into the apple.

Ichabod pulled his dripping face from the
water. He displayed the apple proudly in his
mouth. Then he set the apple down. "I got one!
I got one!" he declared.

"Wonderful!" Katrina cried. An old farmer
and his son laughed and clapped.

Brom Bones strutted into view. His friends
Hans and Dieter were right beside him. *Those three
always seem to travel in a pack, with Brom as the lead
dog,* Ichabod observed. Brom looked around the
enclosed porch, then approached the table.

"Hello, Brom," Katrina said, dimples appear-
ing in her pink cheeks as she smiled. "Would you
like to try bobbing for apples?"

Brom stared down at the bucket and smiled. "No, I'd rather not," he replied.

"It's very easy, Brom," Katrina explained. "Anyone can do it."

Brom looked at Ichabod, then grinned. "I have no desire to have an apple stuck in my mouth like a roasted pig."

Hans and Dieter laughed.

Ichabod sat up on his haunches and shook the water from his fur. "Oh, Brom, you really should give it a try," he urged. "The Van Tassels have gone to great lengths to entertain us. It is only polite to take part in their games. How about one little bob?"

Brom only shook his head. With a dismissive wave of his hand, he, Dieter, and Hans went back inside the house.

Katrina shrugged and turned back to the apple-bobbing bucket. Ichabod placed his paws alongside the bucket again and beamed up at Katrina. "Oooh! Let's see if I can bob and get another one!"

Chapter Twelve

Ichabod bobbed for apples several more times. His skill improved with each round. He gobbled down each new apple he snagged before bobbing for the next. Soon a towering pile of apple cores rose beside the bucket.

"Would you care to try, Katrina?" Ichabod asked.

Katrina smiled and shook her head. "No, I must greet our guests. I see that several more people have arrived."

"I'll join you!" Ichabod leaped down from the table.

Katrina laughed. "I think you need to dry off first," she told him.

All this bobbing for apples has left my fur quite damp, Ichabod realized. "Well, perhaps you are right. I will find a nice fireplace while you attend to your other guests. Please save more dances for me," he said.

"I shall!" Katrina promised. She and Ichabod reentered the house. Katrina joined a group of bouquet-carrying young men just inside the front door.

Ichabod went in search of a cozy fireplace so he could dry off. He trotted through the large house and found a group of people sitting on a wooden bench in front of a huge fireplace in the back parlor. Brom Bones leaned against the mantel, listening to the conversation. Ichabod flopped onto the rug in front of the fire and laid his nose on his paws.

"You know," Mrs. Van Kavner said, "we are a bit overdue for another sighting of the Headless Horseman."

Her husband glanced at her, one eyebrow raised. "Is it that time of year again?"

She nodded firmly. "Oh, yes. I keep track of these things. After all, it is All Hallow's Eve—Halloween."

"What do you think, Ichabod Crane?" Mr. Van Kavner asked.

Ichabod scrambled to his four feet, walked over to the bench, and sat down next to Mrs.

Van Kavner. "Oh, I agree! The signs are all around. Why, just the other evening, my schoolhouse was turned completely upside-down by a poltergeist."

A gasp went through the room. Brom shook his head and grinned, but Ichabod continued.

"That activity itself could be a sign that more strange ghosts are yet to come. Perhaps we will even have a visit from the Headless Horseman!"

Ichabod noticed Katrina standing by the doorway.

"Don't you agree, Katrina?" he asked.

Katrina glanced behind her, toward the music and the laughter coming from the room behind her. "I'm tired of all these stories," she complained. She smoothed the front of her party dress, then twisted a ribboned braid between her fingers. "Won't you come dance with me, Ichabod?" she asked.

"Uh . . . just a moment, dear." Ichabod turned to Brom. "What are your thoughts, Brom?"

Katrina rolled her eyes, then spun on her heels and left the room.

"It's a bunch of nonsense, if you ask me," Brom replied.

Ichabod stared at the man, his round brown eyes wide with surprise. *The great Brom Bones is so foolish as not to believe in all these tales? Astonishing!*

Everyone else stared at Brom, as well. They were speechless with shock. *I can't wait to hear him explain himself,* Ichabod thought.

"I mean, give me something I can touch or hit if I want to," Brom continued. "The spirits are just that—spirits!"

Exactly! Ichabod thought. *Spirits are spirits—which is just the reason why they are so scary! If they were just ordinary people, we'd have nothing to fear.*

"Spirits can do no more harm than a summer breeze," Brom declared.

"Old Man Brouwer didn't believe in ghosts and spirits, either," Mrs. Van Kavner said. "That is, until the Headless Horseman nearly had him! Brouwer told me that the Horseman kidnapped him and took him all the way to the old church bridge! Lucky for Brouwer that the Horseman was unable to cross that bridge."

Why, that's the very bridge I crossed to come here tonight! Ichabod realized, his fur bristling. *The one near the church and the cemetery.*

Brom frowned and said, "Ah! Brouwer is a drunk."

Ichabod cocked his head, studying Brom. "It surprises me that a man of your importance cannot see the significance of these signs," he told Brom. To Mrs. Van Kavner, he said, "Tell me more of Brouwer's story."

Mrs. Van Kavner shuddered. "Oh, it was terrible! I would have fainted on the spot. That's what I would have done."

The group huddled closer together.

Mrs. Van Kavner continued her story in a low voice. "The Headless Horseman came upon Old Man Brouwer in Sleepy Hollow just at the midnight hour. The evil creature forced Brouwer up onto its demon horse!"

"No!" Ichabod gasped.

Mrs. Van Kavner nodded. "He sat right behind the creature! Oh, what a ride it was! They galloped over hills and through valleys, over dry land and swamp. Then they reached the bridge." She shut her eyes, as if to keep away the terrifying sight.

"What happened then?" Ichabod asked in a whisper.

Mrs. Van Kavner opened her eyes again. They glittered in the firelight. "They reached the church bridge. There, right in front of Brouwer, mere inches away, the Headless Horse-man turned into a skeleton!"

Ichabod's heart thumped. His tail wagged as he imagined this terrifying change.

"This skeleton had the strength of ten men," Mrs. Van Kavner continued. "It threw Brouwer from his horse. The poor man landed in the stream. He watched the huge horse spring away over the treetops in a clap of thunder."

What a story! Ichabod's heart thumped harder with excitement. "So the Horseman is never able to cross the bridge?" he asked. "That's useful to know."

Brom laughed. "You call yourself an educated man?" he asked Ichabod. "All you're doing is sitting around, telling fairy tales."

This bully knows so little! "I assure you," Ichabod replied, "it is very important to learn all you can about a spirit. Then you can take the proper steps to keep it away!"

"I tell you this," Brom declared. "If I should meet up with the Headless Horseman, I shall challenge him to a race! My Daredevil can overtake any horse—especially one that is no more than a spirit!"

"Take care," Ichabod warned, glancing around. "Ghosts are known to eavesdrop. You may find yourself having to live up to your boast!" With his paw, he patted the little anti-witch bell dangling from his vest for courage. *Yup,* he thought, *still there, right where I put it.*

"Ha!" Brom exclaimed. "I'm not here for superstitious nonsense. I'm here for the party!" Without another word, he went into the next room.

Ichabod shook his head. "Brom Bones may one day regret his ignorance," he said.

"You could be right," Mr. Van Kavner said. "I heard of one poor farmer who did challenge the Horseman."

"Really?" Ichabod said, his ears pricking up. "What happened?"

"The gentleman in question had returned from the neighboring village of Sing-Sing when the Headless Horseman made an appearance. Well, this lad was quite foolish—like our friend Brom," Mr. Van Kavner added with a nod toward the next room. "He challenged the apparition to a race for a bowl of punch. The two were running neck and neck, finally arriving at the church bridge. But the moment the demon horse's hooves stamped onto the first plank, the Horseman vanished in a fiery flash."

"What happened to the young man?" Ichabod asked.

Mr. Van Kavner shook his head. "He was never quite the same after the race. He has long since left Sleepy Hollow."

"I once caught a glimpse of the Headless Horseman's horse," Mrs. Van Kavner admitted.

"And where did *you* see the frightening creature?" Ichabod asked.

"It was tied to the fence that borders the graveyard next to the church," Mrs. Van Kavner told Ichabod.

I can well imagine that church should be a favorite spot for troubled apparitions, Ichabod thought. *It is so isolated. And the path leading to the bridge is shadowed by towering trees, so sunlight can barely filter through. A gloom sits over it even during days with the brightest daylight.*

Ichabod and the little group huddled on the bench, comparing notes about the headless rider. Outside the wind moaned, and the bare tree branches beat against the windows as the moon rose high in the Halloween sky.

Why, each story is more fur-raising than the last, Ichabod noted, as the storytellers shared their terrifying tales in hoarse whispers.

Ichabod glanced around and saw other

guests eating and dancing. *Perhaps I should go back to Katrina,* he thought. Then Mrs. Van Kavner began to tell another scary tale. *Well, just one more story,* he decided. *Then I'll make like a party animal again.* He jumped from the bench and lay back down in front of the fire.

Ichabod leaped up at the sound of footsteps entering the room. His heart beat a bit faster until he realized the new arrival was none other than his host, Mr. Van Tassel.

"All right, folks," Mr. Van Tassel announced. "It is time for you to go to your own homes."

Ichabod glanced around and realized that the fire had burned down so low it was nearly nothing but ashes. He and Mr. and Mrs. Van Kavner were the only guests still remaining.

"Oh, dear," Mrs. Van Kavner said. "Look how late it has become."

Ichabod yawned and stretched his four legs. He had been sitting for such a long time that his furred limbs were stiff. He looked around. "Where is Katrina?" he asked Mr. Van Tassel.

"She went to bed hours ago," Mr. Van Tassel answered. "It's past midnight."

Ichabod's fur bristled. "Past midnight?" he repeated. *Uh-oh. This isn't good. Past midnight on All Hallow's Eve. I'd say I couldn't come up with a more unlucky time for traveling if I tried!*

Ichabod trotted over to a window and looked out. The wind moaned and whistled. The scraggly tree branches waved, and a few loose wooden shutters slammed against the house.

Mrs. Van Kavner shuddered. "I'm glad I don't have to go through Sleepy Hollow on a night like this. Our home is in the opposite direction." She stood and walked over to her

husband. She then wrapped her shawl more tightly around herself.

Her husband patted her shoulder to calm her. Then he turned to Ichabod. "Say, Ichabod," he said. "Don't you pass through Sleepy Hollow on your way home?"

"Why . . . uh . . . yes," Ichabod replied, trying to keep the fear out of his voice.

Mr. and Mrs. Van Kavner exchanged a worried look. Then Mrs. Van Kavner gave Ichabod a bright smile. "Well, if anyone can handle the Headless Horseman, it is Ichabod Crane," she said.

"I can?" Ichabod gulped. "I mean, of course I can!" He trotted toward the front door, then stopped. "I *think* . . ." he added under his breath.

Ichabod knows he has to face the dark night, even though he is scared.

Joe also has to face something that frightens him.

Well, with me by his side, I'm sure that Joe can handle any trouble in his path . . . even the supernatural kind.

I hope . . .

Chapter Thirteen

"Oh, no," Joe murmured. "*Anything* but this." Wishbone stood on the sidewalk beside Joe and stared up at the old, abandoned Murphy house. Joe looked down at the clue he held in his hand. Sam and David stood on either side of him. He crumpled the paper and dropped it to the ground.

"Are you sure this is the right address?" Wishbone asked. "It doesn't exactly look as if a tea party is going to be held here." He glanced up at Joe. "Well, you don't look happy about being here," he observed.

"This isn't good," Joe said in a low voice.

Bang! Everyone jumped as a broken shutter hit the peeling side of the house. The old Murphy place loomed silently in front of them, hidden almost completely by shadows and a lot of over-grown weeds. Two jack-o'-lanterns sat grinning on the porch. The candlelight inside them flickered, making them look as if they were winking.

"Okay," Wishbone said. "Is it just me, or did things just get really spooky?"

A small figure dressed in silver ran toward them.

"Hey, look!" Wishbone said. "It's Jimmy."

"I'm not going in! I'm not going in!" Jimmy exclaimed as soon as he came up to the group. "He went in, but I'm not going in."

"Do you mean that Damont's already in there?" Sam asked.

Jimmy nodded. "He's been in there a really long time," Jimmy told them.

"Oh, no!" Sam groaned. "Quick, guys! Let's go!" She went through the broken-down gate and into the overgrown yard. Then she stopped and turned around. "Come on!" she urged. "What are you waiting for? Damont is going to beat us to the grand prize!"

Wishbone, David, and Joe stood on the pavement, looking at her. Finally, Joe answered, "I can't."

Sam looked puzzled. "What do you mean, you can't?"

David glanced at Joe, then at Sam.

"It's haunted," David explained. "The house is haunted."

"Haunted? I knew there was something I didn't like about this place," Wishbone said. "No wonder that sneaky black cat wants to hang around here."

Sam shook her head. "It's just the old Murphy place. I'm sure it's safe."

"It's *not* safe," Joe said. He shuddered slightly. "Believe me, I know."

Wishbone began to back away from the house. "Joe's word is good enough for me, folks" he said. "Let's go home and have some of Ellen's cookies."

"He's right," David said.

"Of course I'm right," Wishbone responded. Then he realized David was referring to Joe. "So you agree with Joe, David?" Wishbone asked. "You think the house is haunted, too?"

"What?" Sam asked, confused.

"I knew it!" Jimmy exclaimed. "I told Damont that it was haunted. I did, but he didn't listen. I told him it was probably full of—"

Sam glanced over at Joe. "Jimmy," she said quickly. "Enough! Okay?"

Jimmy nodded and became silent.

Sam turned to Joe. "Now, what are you talk-ing about?"

"Yeah, Joe, tell us what's going on," Wish-bone said. "I don't think I've ever seen you like this. Something really scary must have happened to have you so spooked."

Joe took a deep breath and glanced at David. So far, Joe had been able to avoid the Murphy house. But now it seemed his luck had just run out. *It figures,* he thought. *This is just the way I expected a Halloween night to go.*

David nodded encouragingly, and Joe let out a sigh. *I should get this off my chest,* he thought.

Joe could see a look of concern on Sam's face. *I'd better start talking, or Sam's going to think it's a lot worse than it is,* he told himself. *In fact, it seems almost silly to talk about. Only it didn't seem silly at the time.* The fear Joe felt as he stood gazing at the Murphy house was totally serious.

"It happened a long time ago," Joe began. "It was the first Halloween that my mom let me go trick-or-treating without her." He remembered how he had asked his mom over and over to be allowed to go out on his own. He felt he was too big to have to be taken everywhere by his mom. If only he had known how that night was going to turn out.

"David and I went all over the neighborhood that night," he continued. He glanced over at David. "Some kids talked about going to Thunder Road."

"I was the one who wanted to go," David added.

"Thunder Road?" Wishbone repeated. "That's where we are right now!"

"Where was I?" Sam asked.

"And why don't I remember this?" Wishbone wondered.

"You were on that trip with your mom," David explained. "Remember? And Wishbone didn't go with us, because he was still a puppy."

Wishbone smiled.

The whistling wind blew Sam's blond hair onto her shoulder and she brushed it back. "What happened?" she asked.

Joe glanced around. "It was windy that night, too. But there was also lightning."

He shivered and then shoved his hands deep into his pockets. It was easy to picture that windy night. . . .

"The house didn't seem that bad from the street," Joe remembered. "So I walked toward the place."

Slowly, slowly, Joe remembered he had headed up the overgrown path. The wind had howled around him. Trees had seemed to reach toward him.

"The closer I got, the worse the place looked." Joe's heart began to pound harder, just as it did all those years ago. The memory of the experience was so clear even now. "And the noises! Thunder. Creaks and moans. I didn't think I could do it. But I had to. I wasn't going to turn back. Not in front of David."

"Too bad you didn't have your brave and faithful dog with you," Wishbone said. "Then it would have been easy!"

Joe recalled the flashes of lightning that had made him jump. They had created terrifying shadows across the front of the house. "I reached out to grab the doorknob," Joe continued, "when—*bam!*—the door suddenly blew open."

To this day, he wasn't sure how that door had opened. Maybe it *was* the wind, but how could . . . ? Joe shook his head hard and shut his eyes, but the scene had been drawn forever in his memory. The creepy feeling suddenly threatened to overtake him even now. He took a deep breath.

"There, when I went inside, was a pair of flaming orange eyes, staring right at me!"

"Wow!" Sam murmured.

Joe gave a nervous laugh. "I've never been so scared in my life. Believe me, I ran out of there so fast I could have won a medal for sprinting!" He could still feel those strange eyes digging right into him. His hands began to feel clammy.

"Spooky!" Wishbone shivered under his fur.

"Why did you go there in the first place?" Sam asked.

David gazed at his shoes. He scuffed his sneaker toe on the sidewalk. "I dared him," David finally admitted.

"I-I don't think I can go back in there now," Joe said. He shook his head. "It's just my luck that the final clue should lead us here. On Halloween, no less."

A scream from inside the Murphy house startled them all.

"What's that?" Wishbone demanded, his fur bristling.

A gust of wind blew open the door. Then, with a hiss, the black cat dashed out of the tall grass and ran into the dark house. In a flash, Wishbone took off after it.

"Joe!" he called. "It's the cat! Come on! We've got him trapped inside!"

"Wishbone, no!" Joe shouted.

Wishbone dashed onto the porch and into the house. He was determined to catch the cat. *You're not getting away from me this time, kitty,* he promised. *You're not going to bring any more bad luck tonight. If you can go into this old house, so can we! Joe and I can handle anything a cat can.*

"Oh, no," Joe murmured to his friends. "It's not safe in there. Anything could happen to Wishbone." With a shake of his head, Joe raced toward the Murphy house. David and Sam ran just steps behind him.

Jimmy sat down beside the crooked fence. "I'm not going in there," he called after them.

Maybe not, Joe thought to himself as he hesitated on the threshold of the gloomy and haunted house, *but I guess* we *are.*

Sam ran back to Jimmy. "Here, use my flashlight if you want to," she offered.

Jimmy smiled at Sam. She smiled back and returned to the house.

Chapter Fourteen

Joe came to a sudden halt the moment he crossed the creaking threshold of the Murphy house. He could feel his heart pounding, and he knew it wasn't because of that quick sprint across the lawn.

I'm actually inside this place, he thought, as his eyes adjusted to the darkness. He took a deep breath. *Stay cool,* he told himself. Wishbone might need him. He could feel sweat dripping down his forehead.

Sam and David stepped up behind Joe.

"Wow!" Sam said. "Look at this place."

"It's even worse than I remembered," Joe said under his breath. *Don't press the panic button,* he ordered himself. *The house is just decorated for Halloween. Mr. Del Rio sure did a great job.* Joe shook his head. *Too bad that doesn't make me feel any better.* . . .

"Here, kitty, kitty," Wishbone called into the darkness of the house. He heard Joe, Sam, and David enter the house behind him. "Sorry, Joe," he said, trotting over to join them. "He got away from me again."

Joe and his friends stood in the front hall-way, staring at their surroundings.

"What are you all looking . . . ?" Wishbone scanned the room. It was almost pitch-black, and the torn curtains and broken shutters allowed the full moon to cast strange shadows throughout the dark entryway. A rolling fog blew down the rickety staircase from the second floor.

Where is that coming from? Wishbone wondered as he watched the thick mist float toward them down the stairs. It poured through the slats in the dusty railing, filling the entryway with a cold, bluish haze. Cobwebs hung from the empty light fixtures, chandelier, and door-ways. Wishbone shivered. *It sure is creepy in here,* he thought.

Bang! Wishbone leaped high into the air at

the sound of the door to the house slamming shut behind them. Sam let out a gasp of surprise. Joe shut his eyes tight.

"Well, this has been fun. Can we go home now?" Wishbone asked.

Slowly, Joe opened his eyes and began to breathe normally again.

"It's probably Mr. Del Rio having fun with us," Sam assured Joe. To Wishbone, though, Sam sounded as if she was trying to convince herself, too. "Come on, Joe," she added. "I'm sure there's nothing to be afraid of."

Joe took a deep breath and straightened his shoulders. "Right. I can do this," he said firmly. "Let's get the prize and get out of here."

"Deal," David agreed.

"I'm right behind you," Wishbone said. "You go first."

The group stepped through the doorway that led into the main room. Instantly, faint, eerie green lights clicked on.

"Who turned on the lights?" Wishbone asked. He looked at David, Sam, and Joe. "If none of you did, and I didn't, then who . . . ?" He turned his head around quickly to see if anyone was behind him.

David glanced around the room. "There

must be motion detectors hidden somewhere. They turn on the chandelier above us when anyone enters the room."

"Yeah, I knew that," Wishbone said. He stopped short at the sight of four mummies completely wrapped in gauzy bandages and sprawled in chairs at a table. Dusty teacups and saucers and a teapot draped with cobwebs sat on the table in front of them. "Uh . . . guys? Wishbone said. "We're not alone."

"I think we found the tea party," David told everyone.

Wishbone stared at the mummies. "I guess this is what happens if you wait too long for your snacks."

Sam decided to explore the other side of the room. Wishbone followed her. She knew that Joe was nervous. She wanted to prove to him there was really nothing to be afraid of. In fact, she thought this haunted-house setup was really quite clever. Her team probably still had a chance to win the grand-prize gift certificate.

Sam came to a set of doors with words scrawled in red letters across them. "'Family

Fortune,'" she read aloud, reaching for the door handles. She pulled open the doors—and something leaped out at her.

"A skeleton!" Sam gasped and jumped back, trying to duck out of the reach of the clattering bones swinging toward her.

Wishbone covered his eyes with his paw. "Put it back, Sam!"

Sam took several deep breaths. She shook her head at the skeleton, which now hung crookedly from a closet door. "It's okay, Wishbone," she said. "It's not real."

Wishbone backed up. "I know that," he said. "And you know that. But does the skeleton know that?"

Sam could see that the swinging skeleton was attached to some kind of pulley system, strung with nearly invisible fishing wire. It was rigged so that it would leap out at anyone opening the door.

Sam patted Wishbone. Then she straightened her pith helmet. *I can imagine why Joe thinks this place is haunted. But, don't let this place get to you,* she told herself.

"What else is going to jump out at us?" Wishbone wondered. He trotted alongside Sam as they rejoined David and Joe in the center of the large room.

David glanced over Sam's shoulder, and a puzzled expression crossed his face. "Hey," he said, pointing to the tea party setup. "Wasn't that mummy just sitting over there?"

"You mean they're moving around while we're not watching?" Wishbone asked. "And I thought the black cat was sneaky!"

"Look at this!" Joe reached over to a small side table and picked up a bright orange napkin.

"What?" Sam asked.

"It's a clue," Joe explained. He took the napkin over to the fireplace and held it up to the flickering candle sitting on the mantel. "It says, 'The green player will show you the light.'"

"We could use some stronger light in here," Wishbone said.

"'Green player'?" David said. He glanced around. "I don't see anyone playing anything."

Suddenly, a loud thud from upstairs made them all tense up again. All of Wishbone's sharp senses went on high alert.

"What was that?" David asked, gazing upward at the ceiling. He sounded nervous.

"I-I don't know," Joe stammered.

"Well, I do!" Sam told them. "Damont!"

Wishbone's ears stood up at the mention of Damont's name. "Oh, *really?*" He dashed back into the front hallway. "All right, Damonster," he called up the stairs. "I'm ready for you."

Wishbone looked through the fog that streamed down the stairway.

"Trying to scare my buddy, are you?" the dog challenged. "Ready or not, I'm coming up there!"

With that, Wishbone raced up the creaking staircase to the second story of the Murphy house!

I'm the kind of dog who leaps to meet any challenge!

Ichabod is a little more hesitant to do so. Still, he bravely heads out into the gloomy Halloween night. . . .

Chapter Fifteen

Ready or not, here I go, Ichabod thought as he stared into the dark night.

"Nothing should scare the intelligent and brave Ichabod Crane," Mr. Van Tassel said, leading Ichabod to his horse.

The Van Kavners had already climbed into their carriage and were heading along the road in the opposite direction from Sleepy Hollow.

"I imagine you would be able to show those spirits a thing or two," Mr. Van Tassel told Ichabod.

"Er . . . um . . . yeah, sure, whatever you say," Ichabod mumbled. Mr. Van Tassel held the reins as Ichabod leaped up into the saddle. Ichabod hoped that Gunpowder would be in a cooperative mood. Gunpowder gazed around sleepily, chewing on a strand of hay. Ichabod took the reins from Mr. Van Tassel and held them tightly in his teeth. He gave them a sharp snap to get the horse in motion. Then he began the long journey home.

Why, it is the witching hour, he realized with a pinch of fear.

The moon hung low and full in the dark sky, and glittering stars twinkled brightly. But they did not hold back the darkness. Suddenly, gusting winds blew dark clouds across the night sky. The clouds blotted out the stars and moonlight, plunging Ichabod and Gunpowder into pitch-blackness. Each time another cloud crossed in front of the moon, Ichabod's paws clutched tightly on the pommel of the saddle, and his teeth clenched the reins even more tightly than before.

Why did I have to stay so long at the party? Ichabod asked himself. *I could have been home asleep by now, curled up in my warm bed, my ears flopped onto my soft pillow. Now look at the trouble I'm in.*

Ichabod shivered, remembering how fur-tingling the ghost stories had become by the time most of the guests had gone home. *That Mrs. Van Kavner is like an encyclopedia of supernatural knowledge! She must know every haunted* spot in all of Sleepy Hollow, as well as in the surrounding villages.

Ichabod glanced fearfully around. He knew that many of Mrs. Van Kavner's tales took place all along the route he was riding.

"Giddap!" he urged Gunpowder. The poor animal continued to plod along the trail. "Come on! Giddap, I say!"

But the horse ignored its rider. Ichabod knew he was in for a very long journey. *This horse is making all local stops,* he thought.

Ichabod tried to keep his eyes on the path straight ahead. Yet somehow he could not help but glance over at the gigantic tree from which the unfortunate Major Andre had been hanged.

How can I not stare at that tree? he thought. *It towers over the road.*

Indeed, the gnarled and twisted limbs seemed to reach straight out toward Ichabod. The branches were thick enough to be tree trunks themselves. The tree had an ugly, depressing presence. Ichabod would have guessed that it was haunted, even if Katrina had not told him its gloomy history.

Ichabod began to whistle. *Just to keep myself company.* His voice shook as he sang a few notes. Then he quickly fell silent. *What's that?* His ears pricked up. *Do I hear a fellow whistler?* His ears flopped back down into their relaxed position when he realized the whistling he had heard was only the sounds of the late-night wind.

He looked at Major Andre's tree and felt his heart thump a little faster. *Something white! There— standing out against the blackness of the tree trunk! What can it be?* He gazed fearfully at the tree as he rode past it. *Ah, it's just a spot where the bark has peeled off the trunk. No doubt it's the result of having been struck by lightning. All perfectly normal. Nothing supernatural about that!*

Ichabod must have nervously flicked the reins, because the horse actually picked up a little speed. *Either that, or the horse is aware of spirits in the area. Animals are very sensitive to all things supernatural. Don't think about that,* he scolded himself. *Just be grateful that the horse is moving more quickly.*

One ghost down, how many more to go? Ichabod wondered. *What of the most terrifying spirit of all? Will the dreaded Headless Horseman make an appearance tonight?*

"Oh, dear, oh, dear," Ichabod whispered. "What new dangers lie up ahead?"

I still have to make my way over the haunted stream, through Wiley's Swamp, then into the very

heart of Sleepy Hollow—right into the heart of Headless Horseman territory.

Gulp. "Are we at the stream already?" Ichabod asked.

That meant he would have to guide Gunpowder across the little bridge into the marshy swamp. If only he could convince the horse to move a little faster. Ichabod kicked the horse with a hind leg. To his shock, Gunpowder responded. Instead of going straight, however, the horse lurched sideways.

"I see you are not used to riders and their instructions," Ichabod said. He tugged the reins sharply in the other direction. He didn't want to end up half on and half off the bridge. But this movement seemed to confuse Gunpowder even more.

Every moment I delay is another chance for the spirits to surround me, Ichabod realized. Fear rose in his chest. *I must get this beast moving!* He kicked the horse again. Finally, Gunpowder made it over the planks and to the other side of the stream.

Ichabod was now in the very thick of Sleepy Hollow. He noticed that the trees seemed to grow closer together on this side of the stream. The sky itself seemed darker, as if the stars were farther away and the moon was fading.

"Aargh!" Ichabod shrieked, as Gunpowder came to a sudden stop. Ichabod was flung forward hard. He had to grip the horse's tangled mane in his paws to keep from being thrown to the ground. He could feel the horse trembling beneath him. *Uh-oh,* he thought. *That's not a good sign.*

Ichabod turned his head around quickly at the sound of a rooster crowing in the distance. *That's not a good sign, either! A rooster crowing just after midnight is a terrible omen.*

"Come on, Gunpowder, please, please, *please,* get a move on!"

But for the moment the horse was too frightened to move.

What should I do? Ichabod's heart pounded faster and faster. *Should I simply get down from the horse and lead him the rest of the way? That could take hours,* he realized.

Splish. Splish. Splish.

"What's that?" Ichabod gasped. This time, the shivering that went from his nose to his tail told him he wasn't imagining things. Something—or someone—was edging along the swampy marsh.

"Hello?" he called.

No answer.

"Nothing," Ichabod whispered to himself. "It's nothing."

Then he heard another sound—even closer.

Ichabod's fur bristled. He sniffed the air, trying to catch a scent. The sound from the swamp had moved. Now it was coming from the bushes. Whatever it was, it was headed his way.

It sounded very much like a horse's hooves.

No doubt about it, Ichabod thought. *I am not alone!*

The situation is getting very terrifying for Ichabod in Sleepy Hollow.

Pretty scary events are taking place in Oakdale, too!

Chapter Sixteen

"Okay, Damont," Wishbone challenged, "you want to turn this into a game of hide-and-seek? I have to warn you, I'm one dog with a nose for sniffing out even the most secret hiding places."

As he reached the top of the stairs, the terrier had trouble figuring out which way to go. The fog blurred his usually fine vision and interfered with his sense of smell.

The second floor is as creepy as the first floor, Wishbone noticed. He gazed at the shadowy doorways, creaking floorboards, and cobwebs hanging everywhere. *Now, where did Damont go?* he wondered. "Come out, come out, wherever you are!" he called.

Aha! Just as Wishbone passed an open door,

he thought he caught Damont's scent. He went inside the room and into a closet, only to discover it was empty, except for a few articles of clothing hanging from the rod. *Well, Damont may not be here now,* Wishbone thought, sniffing the floor, *but he's been here recently. I am on the trail!*

He turned to follow the scent when—*wham!*—the door slammed in his face.

"Whoa!" he exclaimed. "I nearly lost my nose there." He pushed at the door with his paw, but it didn't budge. "Trapped!" he gasped. He pushed again, but it was no use.

Okay, what does a dog do in a case like this? He makes as much noise as possible! Wishbone stood on his hind legs, leaned his front paws against the door, and barked. And barked. And barked some more.

Okay, I've tried barking, howling, yapping, yipping, and general noise-making, he thought. *When is someone going to let me out?*

Finally, the door opened. Joe, Sam, and David stared down at him.

"Gosh!" Wishbone said, trotting out of the closet. "What took you so long? I went through my entire vocal range!"

"How did you get in there?" Joe asked.

"Somebody shut the door on me," Wishbone explained. A quick movement caught his eye. *The cat!* "Aha! It's you again! Did you have something to do with this?" He raced after the cat, dashing back down the stairs.

"Wishbone!" Joe called. "Stop!"

Wishbone could hear footsteps behind him on the stairs, but he didn't glance back. He was going for that cat. A door slamming upstairs made his ears prick up, but he didn't allow that to distract him.

The cat is sneaking around on the ground floor somewhere, Wishbone thought, *and I'm going to find him!*

Damont peeked out of the doorway. He watched as Joe and Sam raced down the flight of stairs after Wishbone.

"You guys led me to the first clue," he told himself, "and now I'll let you lead me to the prize."

Damont was about to step out of his hiding place. Suddenly, he noticed that David was still looking into the closet.

What is David doing? Damont wondered. He watched David step into the closet. It was obvious there was something inside that had caught the boy's attention. *Now's my chance!* Damont told himself. Being careful not to make any noise, Damont crept softly toward David.

David shoved his mad-scientist glasses on top of his head. He looked into the closet. He thought he noticed something written on the back wall. *It could be a clue!*

These old houses sometimes have secret rooms, he thought. *Or secret panels.*

David moved aside the old-fashioned clothing hanging from the rod. There was just enough light to read the words. "'Dead end,'" he muttered, reading the dripping red letters.

Wham! The door suddenly shut behind him. "What . . . ?" David quickly tried to turn the knob. He tried it again. *Oh, no! I'm locked in!*

With a quick flick of his wrist, Damont locked the closet door, trapping David inside.

"Hey!" David called from inside the closet. "What's going on?" The doorknob rattled as David tried to release the lock, but it was no use.

That lock may be old, Damont thought, *but it still works.*

"One down, two to go," Damont murmured under his breath. A slow smile of satisfaction crossed his face as he listened to David banging on the inside of the closet door. Glancing around to be sure that no one had seen him, Damont then headed down the back stairs, quiet as a cat.

There sure are a lot of doors in this place, Wishbone noticed. He wandered back into the main room, where the mummies sat at their tea party.

"That's okay. Don't bother to get up," Wishbone told them. "I'm just passing through here, looking for a certain cat. I don't suppose you've seen him, have you? Oh, right, you're all the strong, silent type."

He crossed the room and then went into the library. There he sat in the middle of the floor and looked around. Flickering in the drafty room were many candles, which made strange shadows dance across the walls.

As Sam and Joe followed Wishbone into the

library, more creepy green lights came on. Wishbone realized David wasn't with the kids. . . . *Hmm, I wonder if that means trouble.*

"What's in here?" Joe wondered. He and Sam glanced around the library.

"More cobwebs and dust," Sam said.

"Hey! Check it out," Joe said. He crossed over to a table with a Chinese checkers game set up on it. A green light shone straight down onto the game board, making it brighter than anything else in the room. "This has to be some kind of clue," he figured.

Sam joined Joe by the Chinese checkers game and dug her hand around in her pocket. She pulled out the green marble that had been in the pumpkin clue at the previous game. She studied the board for a moment. "All the holes are full, except for this one." Sam placed the little green marble into the empty space on the board. "Look," she said. "It matches the others perfectly."

Joe nodded, but then he looked puzzled. "Okay, but now what do we do?"

"We go after the cat!" Wishbone exclaimed. He spotted the black creature slinking across the other side of the room.

A loud knocking sound from upstairs

caused Sam and Joe to jump. Then they stared up at the ceiling. "What was that?" Sam gasped. "Hey! Where is David?"

"Kitty! Stop!" Wishbone raced out of the room as he chased after the cat.

"Oh, Wishbone! Not again!" Joe said.

Joe and Sam raced after Wishbone and ended up in the front hallway. "Now, where did Wishbone go?" Joe wondered as he glanced around.

Joe and Sam had followed Wishbone behind the staircase. Joe popped his head through the open doorway leading down into the pitch-black basement.

"Wishbone?" Joe called. "Are you down there?" He really hoped not.

Joe took a step onto the landing at the top of the basement stairs. He listened for a moment. When he was certain Wishbone wasn't in the basement, he checked out the hallway by the stairs again.

Sam was standing in front of another door, which was opposite the door leading to the basement. A strange scratching noise was coming from the room in front of her. A nervous expression crossed her face.

"Now what?" Joe said. He glanced at Sam. She stepped aside. "I guess we have to check it out," Joe said. "It's better to know what's behind the door than just to stand here wondering about it." Joe took a deep breath and reached for the doorknob. He turned it and swung the door open wide. . . .

"Thanks, Joe." Wishbone trotted out of the room. "This is really getting on my nerves," he complained. "Who keeps slamming doors around here?"

Joe shook his head. Then he bent down and patted Wishbone. As he stood up again, he asked, "Where's David?"

"I don't know, but before we do anything else," Sam said, "we should find him."

"I agree," Joe said. "Let's not get separated." Joe stepped into the room where Wishbone had been locked. "Maybe David's in here."

Sam followed a step behind him.

Wishbone noticed a tiny movement behind him, at the door to the basement. He stood there and waited to see if the cat was going to reappear. "No! It's Damont!" he exclaimed.

Wishbone watched Damont sneaking out of the basement as silently as he could. The boy then crept into the hallway, heading toward the room Joe and Sam had just entered.

"I bet he's going to slam that door shut on them!" Wishbone said. "I need to stop him from trapping Sam and Joe in there!"

Before Wishbone could make a move, the cat suddenly dashed past him, ran over Damont's feet, and scampered down the basement stairs.

"Whoa!" Damont cried. Startled by the cat, he stumbled backward through the basement door. As Damont regained his balance on the landing, Wishbone bolted for the door.

"Whoo-hoo!"

Wishbone jumped up and slammed the door shut with his front paws. Then he turned and sat with his back against the door.

"Two for one!" he cried. "Damont *and* the cat! Well, he and kitty should get along just fine!" Wishbone's tail wagged with satisfaction.

Sam and Joe stepped into the hallway. "What's going on out here?" Joe asked, glancing around. "What was that noise?"

"Guess what I did to Damont, guys," said Wishbone proudly.

Then a recognizable voice, although muffled, came from upstairs. "Help!" David shouted. "Help! I'm up here! I'm locked in the closet!"

Sam and Joe raced up the stairs. Wishbone led the way. "This house should have a fire pole, like the one Mr. Del Rio has back at Oakdale Sports and Games," Wishbone said. "It would make all these trips upstairs and downstairs go a lot faster!"

Sam unlocked the closet door and flung it open.

David burst out. Wishbone trotted over to him. "Hey, David, you'll never guess what I did to Damont."

"That's it!" David said in frustration. "I've

had enough! Prize or not, I'm going home!" He headed for the stairs.

Uh-oh. He sounds as if he really means it, Wishbone thought. *And with the way Joe feels about this place, I guess the scavenger hunt is over.*

Wishbone trotted alongside Joe and Sam as they followed David to the stairway. Then the dog's pal did something that surprised him. Joe came to a sudden stop.

"Wait!" Joe cried.

What is it? The cat? Damont? More ghosts? Wishbone walked to where Joe was standing. He poked his head through the slats in the railing in order to see the floor below.

Joe was leaning over the staircase, pointing at the first floor.

"What is it?" Sam asked, coming to stand beside him.

"Look at the floor!" Joe raced down the staircase and pointed out a pattern of light illuminated on the floor. "It looks like the Chinese checkers game!" he exclaimed.

Wishbone's tail wagged at the sound of the excitement in Joe's voice. He dashed down the stairs to check out the scene.

David and Sam joined them at the spot. David peered up at the chandelier that glowed with a mysterious green light. "The shape must be projected by the chandelier," David said.

Joe knelt down beside the light pattern. "The clue said, 'The green player would show you the light.' Sam, didn't you put the green marble right here?" He indicated a spot on the floor.

Sam knelt down beside him, studying the light pattern. "I think so," she replied.

Joe gazed at the pattern a moment more. He squinted his eyes in concentration.

"That's it, Joe!" Wishbone encouraged him. "You're on a roll!" He could see Joe wasn't letting

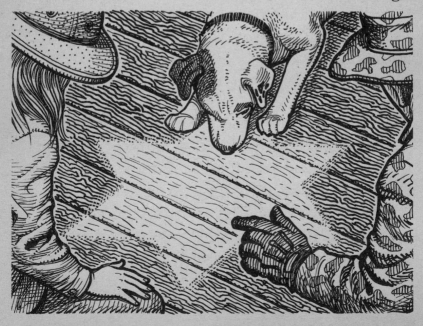

the spooky atmosphere of the Murphy house upset him anymore. "You've got the scent. Now,
follow the trail to the prize."

Joe reached down and felt around the spot
where Sam had placed the marble in the game-
board. With a sharp tug, he yanked up the loose
floorboard. Reaching inside the space, he pulled
out an envelope with the Oakdale Sports &
Games emblem on it.

"Well, look at that," Wishbone said. "I'm
not the only one who buries things around
here."

Joe opened the envelope and pulled out a
piece of paper. "The one-hundred-dollar gift
certificate!" he exclaimed. A broad grin spread
across his face. "We did it!"

Sam smiled at Joe. "*You* did it, Joe," she told
him happily.

"I guess this turned out to be my lucky
night, after all!" Joe said.

David gazed past Joe and looked back into
the main room. "Uh . . . guys," he said with a
shaky voice.

"Huh? What?" Wishbone turned around to
see what was making David so nervous. His
heart thumped a little harder.

Two of the mummies were slowly rising to

their feet. They held their arms out stiffly in front of them. *They seem to be heading right for us!*

"Oh, great," Wishbone said. "Monsters. Just what we need. That's just what tonight was missing!"

Meanwhile, back in Sleepy Hollow, Ichabod has his own monster to face!

Chapter Seventeen

"Hellooooo? Is someone there?" Ichabod called into the darkness. He had to try to find out who was wandering in these woods after the witching hour. No matter how terrifying the stranger's identity might be, Ichabod needed to know who—or what—lurked in the darkness.

Then Ichabod's heart thumped double-time. He knew who must be hiding in the bushes. *No, no, I dare not think it,* he scolded himself. *Put the thought from your mind, Ichabod.*

A large shape appeared from the twisting bushes. It headed over the small planks crossing the stream out of Wiley's Swamp. A *very* large shape. Huge, in fact.

Ichabod's fur stood on end in terror. *It is the*

Headless Horseman! It must be! Oh, dear! Oh, dear! How ever shall I defend myself?

He took several deep breaths to calm down.

Don't jump to conclusions, Ichabod. Perhaps it is only a lost rider needing directions. He looked into the darkness. *Yeah, right,* he thought. *And I'm the Queen of England.*

Still, the schoolmaster hoped that the rider was not a supernatural creature. "Who are you?" Ichabod demanded, his voice shaking with fear.

The shadowy figure remained motionless and silent. Ichabod could sense, however, that the great big shape radiated a lot of power. It stood wrapped in the gloom of night, like a monster ready to pounce upon a traveler.

Ichabod tried again. "Tell me, please, who are you? What do you want?"

Still no response. The silence was almost as terrifying as the strange creature's huge, threatening presence.

Okay, be that way. Ichabod picked up the reins in his teeth again and urged Gunpowder forward. *Enough chitchat—we're outta here.*

Ichabod was relieved to discover that Gunpowder had recovered from his shock. He was now willing to trot along at a quick pace.

Unfortunately, so did the strange and silent creature following Ichabod. Then, moving so quickly that Ichabod felt his fur ruffle, the figure rode ahead of him to the middle of the road.

Ichabod gave a sharp tug on the reins with his teeth. He pulled Gunpowder to an abrupt halt. Ichabod squinted, looking as hard as he could at the dark shape in front of him. He could now see that the horse and rider stood between him and safety.

How shall I pass? Ichabod wondered. *And what does this horseman want? Why doesn't he speak to me?* Ichabod's heart thudded hard. He already knew the answer to that question. That was why his blood ran so cold.

In his heart, Ichabod knew that the mysterious rider was the dreaded Headless Horseman! Ichabod was sure that the spirit had some horrifying plan in mind for him. Ichabod gulped. *Perhaps it involves my head!*

"You, there . . ." Ichabod called. He had no idea what to say after that. So he said nothing.

To Ichabod's shock, the rider moved off the road. *Why is he allowing me to pass? What could he be up to? Well, I'll take the opportunity now, and quickly, before he changes his mind.*

Ichabod and Gunpowder hurried past the

mysterious rider. Ichabod was terrified that perhaps the Horseman was only waiting for him to get within striking range. To his great relief, Ichabod rode by unharmed.

Still, he could not get a clear look at the unknown rider. The Horseman backed up into the cover of trees, deeper into the shadows. It was such a dark night, Ichabod could barely see his white paw on the pommel of the saddle, let alone anything farther away.

Could the Headless Horseman know that I am no stranger to the ways of the supernatural? Perhaps he fears me! Ichabod's tail wagged at the thought. *Maybe our little game is now over,* Ichabod thought, hoped—indeed, prayed. *And now, it's time to rev up the horsepower!* He clucked and flicked the reins, urging Gunpowder into a fast trot.

Oh, no! The Horseman is still following me, he realized. He could hear the horse's hooves echoing those of Gunpowder's. *If the Horseman plans to attack me, why doesn't he just do so?* He was tempted to dare the creature to come and get him, once and for all! But that was not in the Horseman's plans.

Each time Ichabod picked up speed, so did his silent companion. The few times Gunpowder slowed down, the horse behind him changed its pace, as well. On and on they went, paired in a terrifying dance, Ichabod leading, and the silent stranger following Ichabod's every move.

If only he would speak! If I only knew what terrible plans he has in mind for me. Oh, why, why the silence? I cannot stand it.

Then the wind shifted again, blowing the dark clouds away from the full moon. Some dim light was allowed to filter through the thick tree branches.

Ichabod quickly glanced back. There, standing on a low rise, with a patch of bright moonlight shining down upon him, stood the terrifying rider. Ichabod could deny it no longer. His deepest fear was confirmed.

"The Headless Horseman!" Ichabod gasped as he dropped Gunpowder's reins. His heart seemed to stop beating. Terror shot through his limbs, causing all four legs to tremble. He felt his chest tighten. He tried to catch his breath. "The Headless Horseman!"

Now that he could see the Horseman clearly, Ichabod could not tear his eyes away from the creature. It was even more horrifying than anything he had ever imagined. The horse that the spirit sat upon was huge, and it stomped on the ground in fury. Holding the reins was a large man—or, rather, the large *body* of a man.

The rider atop the horse had no head.

A collar stood up stiffly on top of the broad shoulders, but nothing sat above that. A flowing crimson scarf was wrapped around the thick, headless neck. The ghost wore a long, dark cloak that whipped every which way in the strong wind. Moonlight glinted off the buckles of the well-shined boots. With one large, powerful gloved hand, it gripped the horse's reins.

Clutched in the other arm of the dreadful creature was a glowing, round object—the very thing that should have been sitting on his shoulders!

Ichabod shuddered. The object glowed with an inner fire. It seemed to grin a cruel smile, and its eyes glinted in the moonlight and flickered strangely.

The Headless Horseman's horse whinnied like a werewolf howling at the moon. The sound broke the terrible spell that the Horseman seemed to have cast over Ichabod.

He snapped back his head and let out his own howl of terror. "I am outta here!" he shrieked.

Ichabod kicked wildly with his hind legs.

"Gunpowder!" he cried. "Run as you have never run before!"

The pair dashed through the night, with Gunpowder showing remarkable and surprising speed. *He's as scared as I am!* Ichabod realized. *Well, if that gets him moving, it's fine with me!*

"He-yah!" Ichabod cried, urging the old horse to move even faster. "He-yah!" he yelled again, picking up speed.

Gunpowder ran as if he was a creature possessed, and for that Ichabod was grateful. He could hear the thundering hooves behind him, matching Gunpowder's pace stride for stride. They raced at such a speed that the horses kicked up stones and twigs. Ichabod's cutaway coat flew straight out behind him.

"My bell!" Ichabod suddenly remembered his anti-witch bell, dangling from his vest. Ichabod shook his furred body, hoping to make the bell ring louder. But it was no use. The sad truth could not be denied. "The bell's not working!" he moaned in despair, as the Horseman continued his chase.

Ichabod bounced awkwardly in the saddle as Gunpowder stumbled over twigs and bushes.

The horse shied as a sudden gust of wind blew dead leaves into its face. Ichabod felt the saddle slipping underneath him.

"I'm going down!" Ichabod clutched the saddle with his paws. He tried to keep it in place, but his effort was wasted. Ichabod gave up and swung his paws around the horse's neck, allowing the saddle to slide to the ground. *Either that, or I'll fall myself,* he thought.

For a moment, Ichabod wondered how angry Mr. Van Ripper might be at the loss of his best saddle. *Oh, who cares about that!* he scolded himself. *I must stay on my horse, no matter what, or I shall never escape.*

Ichabod clutched Gunpowder's mane in his paws and managed to sit upright. Still the horses charged through Sleepy Hollow. *Has the place magically grown?* Ichabod wondered. *It has never seemed such a distance.*

His heart was pounding so hard that he was sure the creature behind him could hear it. His breath came in strangled gasps. He felt cold with fear from the tip of his nose to his tail. *Oh, I cannot make it! If the Headless Horseman doesn't get me, this terrifying ride will!*

Then—there it was! Up ahead! "Yes! I am safe! The church bridge!" Ichabod exclaimed.

The wonderful bridge that the Headless Horseman could not cross! No bridge had ever looked
so beautiful.

A snort behind Ichabod made him jump.
The Headless Horseman was right behind him. *I
think I can feel the black steed's hot breath.*

"Come on, Gunpowder! I know you can do
it!" Ichabod cried.

The schoolmaster could feel the relief rush
through him as he and Gunpowder raced across
the bridge to safety. The horse's hooves clattered
loudly on the wide wooden boards.

"We did it! Home free!"

Ichabod pulled on the reins with his teeth.
He brought his exhausted horse to a stop. He
turned around to face his pursuer, ready to
cheer in victory. He wanted very much to be

able to have the satisfaction of watching the terrifying ghost disappear.

"I'll have you know, I am wise to the ways of the supernatural!" he called in his loudest voice to the Headless Horseman. "And now it's time for you to vanish."

The enormous black horse paused for a moment on the other side of the bridge.

"Toodle-loo! It's been nice knowing you. Now, scram!" Ichabod shouted.

What's taking so long? Ichabod wondered. *They are supposed to return to their spirit forms. But they still look pretty solid to me. Why aren't the horse and rider evaporating?*

Lightning crackled in the night sky above them. The Headless Horseman's horse reared up. It let out a furious whinny. Then, to Ichabod's horror, the animal hurled itself toward him across the bridge.

"No!" Ichabod screamed. "You can't! The bridge! It can't be!" Shock made Ichabod drop the reins from his mouth. Gunpowder panicked, throwing Ichabod to the ground. Ichabod lay low, stomach to the ground, covering his eyes with his paws. The Headless Horseman thundered toward him.

Shivering in terror, Ichabod peeked through

his paws. The Headless Horseman crossed the bridge, stood up in his stirrups, and then held up the glowing object that it had clutched in its arm. Next, he hurled it with all his strength directly at Ichabod!

"Yikes!" Ichabod shrieked, scrambling to his four feet. "Incoming!" He spun around and dashed away, hoping to escape the flying, fiery missile.

"I just know Ichabod was carried off by the Headless Horseman," Mrs. Van Kavner moaned.

"There, there, dear," Mr. Van Kavner said, as he helped his wife step along the planks leading from Wiley's Swamp and into the very heart of Sleepy Hollow.

Gunpowder was discovered without his saddle or his rider at the Van Ripper farm the next morning. He showed no sign of his wild ride the night before. However, the old creature was even more cranky and tired than usual.

When Ichabod did not appear at the farm, Mr. and Mrs. Van Kavner heard the news and decided to go on a search for their missing friend. They were convinced that Ichabod had met a terrible end during his long journey home from the Van Tassels' party. To prove it, they went to Sleepy Hollow to search for clues. In broad daylight, of course.

Mr. Van Kavner spotted something trampled in the muddy dirt. He hurried over to it and discovered it was Van Ripper's saddle.

"Well, there were definitely two riders out here last night," Mr. Van Kavner told his wife. He pointed to the ground. "Look—two sets of tracks."

"And look at this, too," Mrs. Van Kavner pointed out. "Ichabod's hat." Then she bent over and looked at a small object. "And here is his witch-bell."

Her husband went over and joined her. "But what is this?" he wondered. There on the ground was a smashed jack-o'-lantern. Mr. Van Kavner knelt down and examined the pumpkin. "This candle inside has been burned nearly all the way down." He picked up the candle and gazed up at his wife. "But why should anyone have brought a jack-o'-lantern all the way out here to the woods of Sleepy Hollow?"

The sound of horse's hooves made the Van Kavners straighten up. Startled, Mr. Van Kavner dropped the candle. Brom Bones rode

toward them on his enormous black horse, Daredevil. He glanced down at the broken jack-o'-lantern.

"Why, indeed?" Brom said with a laugh. He flicked his reins and then rode off, his laughter echoing through all of Sleepy Hollow.

Ichabod's sudden disappearance was a favorite topic of conversation among the guests at the wedding of Katrina Van Tassel and Brom Bones. Everyone remembered

Ichabod and the terrifying tales that he had told at the All Hallow's Eve party. They were sure that he had had a frightening encounter with the dreaded spirit of the Headless Horseman.

But perhaps the evil twinkle in Brom's eyes, whenever he heard the story, suggested quite a different explanation for the schoolmaster's disappearance.

The stories about Ichabod and the Headless Horseman continued for years. Travelers coming through Sleepy Hollow reported that he was back in his home state of Connecticut, teaching in a fine school, and entertaining everyone with his scary stories. They said that his favorite tale was the one about how he had defeated the Headless Horseman.

But most folks in Sleepy Hollow remained convinced that the unfortunate schoolmaster had been carried off by the ghost.

School was held in a new location, and Ichabod's once-joyful little schoolhouse became deserted and fell into decay. In fact, it was reported to be haunted. People passing by at night would claim to hear a strange singing that always frightened the birds away.

So, in time, Ichabod Crane, lover of ghost stories, became a ghost story himself!

Chapter Eighteen

"There has to be some kind of explanation for this," Wishbone said, as he stared at the two mummies heading toward them. "Uh . . . guys? Any explanation at all . . ."

The wrapped-up creatures walked stiffly toward Wishbone and his friends. Their arms stretched out in front of them, reaching . . . reaching . . .

"Make them go away, Joe!" Wishbone ran behind Joe's legs.

Wishbone peeked through Joe's legs as he watched the mummies come to a stop. They reached up to their faces.

"Joe, they're going to peel off their wrappings! I don't want to see what's under there!"

The mummies dug their fingers under their chins and lifted up their masks. . . . The grinning faces of Melina and Marcus revealed themselves! Sam, David, and Joe burst out laughing.

"Oh, it's you two!" Wishbone said. "I knew it all along."

"Congratulations! You won!" Melina exclaimed.

"Did we scare you?" Marcus asked, smiling happily.

"Nah! Not even for a minute," Wishbone replied. "We were on to you all along!"

"Cool costumes," Sam said.

"It was all Uncle Travis's idea," Melina explained. "He thought it would add an extra-special touch of creepiness."

"It sure did," Joe told him.

"Help me!" a voice called, interrupting them. "Someone! Let me out!"

"It's Damont!" David exclaimed.

"Where's his voice coming from?" Joe asked, looking around.

"Help!" Damont cried out again.

Wishbone's ears pricked up. "Follow me!" he cried. "He's still where I locked him—in the basement." Wishbone dashed to the stairs. The others followed him. Joe opened the door under the stairway that led to the basement.

Damont burst out and ran past all of them. "Get me out of here!" he shouted.

Joe stared down into the dark basement. He was suddenly frozen by a frightening sight. Just as before, on that Halloween night at the Murphy house all those years ago, a pair of gleaming eyes stared right at him. Then, with a loud yowl, the black cat dashed up the stairs and ran out of the basement.

Joe took a startled step back. "It was the cat!" Joe cried.

"What?" Sam asked, puzzled.

Joe watched the cat rush out of the house. "That night—it was the cat that I saw. It was just a cat that scared me. Can you believe that?" He laughed and shook his head. "This house isn't haunted, after all." He grinned broadly at Sam.

"You see!" Wishbone said cheerfully. "There was a reasonable explanation, after all."

Joe gazed around the dark room. Wishbone could tell the Murphy house no longer held any sense of terror for his buddy. Those long-ago ghosts had vanished.

Yup, Wishbone thought with satisfaction. *Those fears are behind Joe now. And I was there to help!*

"Come on," Melina said. "Uncle Travis is waiting outside." She led everyone toward the front door.

Wishbone stayed behind and looked once more down the basement stairs. He was startled to see a pair of flaming orange eyes staring back at him. "Hey! What's that?"

Didn't I see that cat race out of here? If the cat isn't down there, then who—or what . . . ?

Wishbone turned and barked furiously to get the attention of his friends. "Guys! Guys! Come quick! You've gotta see this! Eyes! Just the way Joe described them!"

He glanced back down the stairs. *Huh? Where did those glowing eyes go? They were just there!*

Wishbone heard Joe calling his name. *Maybe I was wrong,* he thought. *The dark can play funny tricks on you.* He trotted toward the front door, where his friends were waiting with Melina and Marcus. *I suppose I could have imagined those eyes. No . . . I know I saw them. I think . . .*

"Is it time to claim our victory?" Wishbone asked Melina and Marcus. "Do you think there will be a hero's feast?"

David, Sam, and Joe walked out the front door behind Melina, Marcus, and Wishbone.

"Feel better?" Sam asked Joe.

Joe nodded. "Now that it's over, yes," he told her.

"Hey! Look at all the people!" Wishbone exclaimed, as he trotted down the sagging front steps of the Murphy house.

A large crowd of costumed kids gathered around Travis Del Rio. Some of them had been members of the other teams participating in the scavenger hunt. Others were just neighborhood friends.

Wishbone noticed that Jimmy was tugging on Damont's sleeve. He also noticed Damont looked pretty shaken. "Why, his face is almost as white as my fur!"

"What happened?" Jimmy asked Damont. "Did you see a ghost? I bet you did. One time, a friend of mine, he went inside a haunted house, and he—"

"Don't say anything else," Damont insisted, cutting him off. "We're going home."

"It couldn't have been that scary," Travis said with a smile.

Damont glanced over at him and raised an eyebrow. "Oh, yeah?" he replied. Then he spun around and stormed off. Jimmy followed him, chattering a mile a minute.

"So long, Damont," Wishbone called. "You can dish it out, but you sure can't take it."

Joe smiled and held up the prize-winning gift certificate for the crowd to see. Everyone cheered and applauded as he, David, and Sam came down the front steps. They hurried over to Travis.

"All right!" Travis said, clapping Joe on the back. "Good job—all of you."

"Oh, it was nothing at all," Wishbone said modestly.

Melina and Marcus gave their uncle a hug.

"Did you kids have fun?" Travis asked them.

"We sure did!" Marcus exclaimed.

"Let's do this every year," Melina added.

"So, congratulations," Travis said to David, Sam, and Joe. "I bet you can think of a lot of things you can use that gift certificate for."

"Squeaky toys!" Wishbone quickly answered. "You can never have too many!"

"Thanks, Mr. Del Rio," Joe said.

"Yes, thanks," David echoed.

"That scavenger hunt was really fun," Sam added. A broad grin spread across her face.

Travis turned around to face the crowd. "Listen up, everyone. There's a party back at Oakdale Sports and Games—and you're all invited!"

The crowd let out another cheer. Everyone began to head back toward the sporting-goods store.

"Finally!" Wishbone exclaimed. "I've had enough tricks for one night. Let's talk treats. Mmm-mmm."

Travis fell into step beside Joe. "Well, Joe, it looks like you're back in the zone, after all."

Joe smiled. "Yes, sir," he said.

"It was your lucky day," Travis added with a grin. "Must be the socks."

"Must be," Joe replied.

Joe bent down and patted Wishbone. The dog licked his friend's face in congratulations.

"That's for solving the clues—and for going into that spooky house in the first place."

"We did really well, didn't we?" Joe said to Wishbone.

"We sure did!" Wishbone agreed.

Joe dashed ahead to catch up with his friends.

Wishbone watched Joe joking and laughing. "All those scary old ghosts have vanished into the Halloween night," Wishbone said with satisfaction.

Wishbone glanced at the sound of a familiar *meow.* The black cat sat on the front porch of the Murphy house, licking its paws.

"We shall meet again, kitty," Wishbone promised. Hearing Joe call his name, Wishbone

turned his head toward him. When he looked back again in the direction of the Murphy house, the cat was gone. "How does he *do* that?"

The terrier looked up at the house. *I'm glad this night had a lucky ending. I'm happy that some of the stranger events turned out to have perfectly logical explanations—just like the strange events surrounding the story of Ichabod Crane.*

Some mysteries never do get solved . . . which is what makes them great stories to tell over and over. In fact, I think this Halloween adventure is one I am going to enjoy telling on many a dark and stormy night in the future!

About Washington Irving

Washington Irving was born in 1783. That same year, the United States and Great Britain signed a formal peace treaty. It brought the Revolutionary War to an official end.

New York City, where Irving lived as a boy, was the first capital of this new nation. A story passed around in the Irving family stated that one of their young women servants followed George Washington into a shop. She held up the infant she was carrying and told the famous military general (and first president of the United States) that the baby had been named for him. George Washington touched the infant's head and gave little Washington Irving his blessing.

While George Washington has been known as "the father of our country," his namesake, Washington Irving, has been called "the father of American literature." He was the first American to gain international success and acceptance as a writer. Some of America's greatest writers of later years were influenced by him.

Irving wrote in many styles and used many fictitious names. He wrote essays about his distant travels, spooky ghost stories, histories, and legends of the Wild West.

Irving had a great appetite for travel. He spent many years in Europe. While there, he served as a U.S. government representative in both England and Spain.

Irving's love of traveling to faraway places began early. "I was always fond of visiting new scenes, and observing strange characters and manners," he wrote in his autobiography, *The Author's Account of Himself.* "Even when a mere child I began my travels . . . to the frequent alarm of my parents. . . . I knew every spot where a murder or robbery had been committed, or a ghost seen."

These experiences, and the legends and folktales he gathered along the way, served the author well. They became the source of his many wonderful stories, which still continue to delight readers today.

About "The Legend of Sleepy Hollow"

Sleepy Hollow is a real place in upstate New York. Washington Irving based this story on legends he heard from local folk when he visited the area. "The Legend of Sleepy Hollow," Irving's most well known short story, originally appeared in *The Sketch Book* in 1820. It has continued to be a popular tale from the time when it was first published. In fact, the tale is so well loved that both Westchester and Columbia counties in New York State claim to have been the locations that originally inspired the story!

There is a wooded area know as Sleepy Hollow in Westchester County, north of the village of Tarrytown. Irving spent time there as a boy. He would certainly have heard all the local legends about the Headless Horseman and the graveyard he haunted. When Irving reached adulthood, he bought a huge house in Tarrytown. The place had once been owned by a wealthy farming family, the Van Tassels—just like Katrina's family in the short story.

However, Irving had a good friend he often visited in Columbia County. This man was a schoolteacher who resembled Ichabod Crane. He also had a romantic rival named Brom. To this day, folks in Columbia County claim their little town is the true setting for the ghost tale. There is even a little schoolhouse that was built in the 1800s named The Ichabod Crane Schoolhouse. Local residents maintain the site as a museum.

No matter where the real location was (Irving could have been inspired by both places!), the well-loved short story has been told in many forms: in plays, on television, in books illustrated by many different artists, and now in this book by Carla Jablonski—with lots of help from Wishbone!

About Carla Jablonski

Carla Jablonski is a writer and actress who lives in New York City. There she often goes to museums or to the theater, runs in Prospect Park, or does research in one of the many public libraries.

One of the things Carla enjoyed the most about writing *The Legend of Sleepy Hollow* was doing the background research. She investigated what it would have been like to have been a child in the 1800s in upstate New York. She also read books about the legends and ghost stories that people told during Washington Irving's time. It was a spooky but fun project!

Carla has taught writing classes, and she has also edited many of the *Choose Your Own Adventure* series of books. The first book she wrote for The Adventures of Wishbone series was *Homer Sweet Homer*, based on *The Odyssey*. She also worked on the *Hardy Boys* digest series. Carla wrote the novelization for the TV show *Calling All Creeps*, based on an R.L. Stine *Goosebumps Presents* book. Her plays have been performed in New York City and Edinburgh, Scotland.

Carla is working on lots of different projects—for both children and adults. Writing for The Adventures of Wishbone series is one of her favorite projects because she loves the combination of the classic story from literature and the modern-day Oakdale plot. When Carla isn't writing or performing, she loves to cook—almost as much as Wishbone loves to eat!